The Judas Gate

© Nick McCarty

ISBN 978-0-9554771-7-1

Text prepared by www.willowebooks.org.uk

THE JUDAS GATE

by

NICK McCARTY

KENELM 2012
London

About the author

Nick McCarty has been a professional writer for more than 40 years.

He has worked mostly for television on series like Bergerac, The Onedin Line, Z-Cars, Dangerfield, Spearhead and The Regiment which are being prepared for publication on Kindle.
He wrote the Anne Boleyn segment of The Six Wives of Henry VIII with Dorothy Tutin in the title rôle and Keith Michell as Henry.

He is an award-winning writer for radio. His original plays and adaptations include A Confidential Agent, A Tale of Two Cities, Hard Times, Zorba the Greek, Far from the Madding Crowd and many others

Previous publications

The Iliad Retold - with illustrations by Victor Ambrus (Kingfisher Books)
Troy, the story of its discovery by Heinrich Schliemann (Carlton Books)
Rome - a brief illustrated history (Carlton Books)
Alexander the Great (Carlton Books)
Fox - Cromwell's Spy
Fox - Assassin
Cats Tales
Dragon's Teeth

Contents

THE JUDAS GATE

Frank was back. The best bomb maker in Ulster meant bad luck for B Company, The Wessex Rangers. They all hated bombers. Twiss said it. 'Just give us the chance and I'd have him up a dark alley with this.' He shook his SLR.

Colour-Sergeant Jackson nailed Twiss up. Proof was what they needed and that meant long watches, checking contacts, waiting. Then the bombs began to go off.

Company-Sergeant Major Gilby walked away from the smoking wreckage of what had once been a car and a man. Frank was back OK.

Chapter One

The afternoon little Geordie Tompkins was killed had been a bastard.

By the time it was all over and the streets had been hosed down, the debris taken away and the area searched by sniffer dogs, by Felix and his bomb-detector equipment, and by an infantry platoon, the men of Six Platoon, Wessex Rangers, had had enough. They were sickened and more, because he was their first this tour and they'd only got twelve days to go before they left the Province and headed back to the comforts of barrack life on Salisbury Plain.

Terry Adams stood shaking in a doorway at the end of the mean terrace of houses. He watched as the crowd beyond the barrier stood silently observing the steam rising from the wreck of the car.

With his SLR crooked under his arm and his fingers under the cold, black, metal barrel of the automatic rifle he stared across the wooden barriers and wondered how many of them were pleased at what had happened. The old

1

woman in the middle house had already been taken away by ambulance. It was her stupidity that caused the kid to lose his life. He'd been afraid that the old cow up the street who'd refused to leave her home would get blown to bits if the car went up. It went up all right and Geordie Tompkins with it.

Private Adams felt sick. There was dirt and grime on the backs of his hands and the filth of the streets on his face. He looked across the barricade and saw some of the men and women smiling as they drifted quietly away. It was all over and another statistic was added to the numbers of dead. They didn't give a monkey's so long as it wasn't them.

Private Twiss nursed his rifle and swore steadily at the stink of explosives, at the stench from the burned-out car and at his own tiredness. He just wanted to get out whole, and sod them all. He glanced across the street to the doorway in which Adams was posted to cover them from the street. Even after they'd scored a hit you never knew if they'd open up with a quick burst of automatic fire while they'd got you pinned down doing the necessary work of checking the area for secondary bombs. Twiss sniffed and spat. They'd pulled in the whole of B Company to nail their man and they still hadn't got him. It'd been a big company operation and they'd still missed the bastard who was responsible and that sodding little soldier goes and gets himself killed. No point. Useless.

Across Northern Ireland the British army kept a web of men based in two major centres and deployed in small groups from these centres in country areas and small towns. The Wessex Rangers had already done two four-month tours in the Province when they had been returned for an eighteen-month garrison based on the Londonderry area.

They'd succeeded in rebuilding some of the contacts

between the army and the civilian population which had so suddenly broken down after a child had been shot during a street riot. The recriminations and accusations that had followed had done nothing to give the civilian population any confidence in the impartiality of the soldiers.

For months now the Rangers had been trying to reconstruct this shattered confidence and had found the work unrewarding and slow. Intimidation from the extremists of both communities, and the general battle-weariness of the whole community, made the work even harder.

In the country the patrols and vehicle checks, the observation posts and the intelligence operations had provided little in the way of success and the men were tired of the never-ending pattern: patrols, sleeping and eating in inadequate locations and the week back in base on guard duties, protecting the families of the soldiers, for the women came too and faced the same tensions their husbands faced day in and day out.

To the men of Six Platoon, the endless patrolling and talking didn't seem to do any good and they wanted either to get out and back to the cushy life in barracks or to get stuck in and nail every bastard who might, just might, be a member of the Provisional IRA or of any of the Loyalist paramilitary groups.

Adams looked back along the street towards the paint factory and saw Six Platoon covering the fire brigade and the ambulances. He glanced across the street and grinned as he saw Colour-Sergeant Jackson chatting to Company Sergeant-Major Gilby. 'Jacko'll be pissed off,' Adams thought. 'He'll want to get off to the new observation post Recce Platoon has set up.' Adams wanted to go too. He hated the streets in Northern Ireland. They were mean, poor and dangerous and seemed to be as deliberately ugly as it was possible to make them. He knew why the people

3

here were fighting and in some ways he thought they were right. But he wasn't paid for an opinion. He was paid to carry the SLR and to know how to use it. That was what it meant to be in Northern Ireland for a soldier and there was never the chance of a mistake that Private Terry Adams was anything but a soldier. Nor Gilby, nor Jackson, nor Twiss either. But poor bloody Geordie Tompkins hadn't had a chance to be one before he got his. Stupid bastard.

The white balconies of the Tidworth barracks sparkled in the sun. The red brick of the Victorian buildings glowed in the afternoon light.

Back in England now, the events of twelve days ago had been eclipsed, for B Company, Wessex Rangers, by the prospect of a two-week leave. They had flown back from Northern Ireland yesterday and after half a day of feverish sorting and unpacking were now assembled in the square for a final word from Major Taylor, their commanding officer.

Countless soldiers had come back from overseas and been dismissed from that square to take their leave. They'd all left mates in the soil of India, South Africa, Gallipoli, France, Germany, Cyprus, Aden, Malaya . . . an endless list of battle honours for an endless list of dead men.

Colour-Sergeant Jackson waited at the side of the square and listened as Major Taylor spoke to the men. Jacko grinned as he watched Company Sergeant-Major Gilby. He'd heard it all before and Jacko knew that he wanted to get off parade and into the Sergeants' Mess as soon as he could. The men were standing at ease and Jacko knew that they too were anxious to get away.

'I want you to know how much I appreciate the way things went in Ireland,' Major Taylor went on. 'Apart from the one incident B Company suffered no casualties and did a good job.'

The men in Six Platoon straightened out of their

4

apathy at the mention of the death. Jacko watched Sergeant Bilinski stiffen a touch. They didn't want to be reminded of what had happened such a short time ago. The OC had read the riot act to the company at the time and they were sore at what he had said about Tompkins. Jackson hadn't been there but Tom Gilby was still angry about it.

'He was only a bloody kid straight out of depot. He didn't know . . . and we aren't there to wet-nurse the bastards,' he had said to Jacko as they took their last drink in Stranmoore Barracks the night before they left Ireland. 'No need for the OC to put the boot in just now. We know what went wrong.' Gilby had sunk his pint and got another in. There had been a lot of talking that last night on camp.

The three hundred men stood on the concrete square under the sun and didn't seem to Colour-Sergeant Jackson to be the same as those he'd seen only twelve days before standing around the wreckage of the car. They were still tired and almost every man had the dull, black rings of sleeplessness under his eyes. But now they were clean and eager to be gone. It was a beginning as well as an end of something.

'We have six weeks to go before we are Spearhead Battalion,' said Major Taylor and reminded them that training, when they came back from leave, would be hard. He was going on too long and the men were becoming restless.

Sergeant-Major Gilby caught Jacko's eye and raised one eyebrow in exasperation. Jacko grinned. He wanted a word with Tom before he went off to join Mary and the kids at her parents' place. He wondered for a moment what Tom Gilby would do with his leave.

'Army bachelor,' Mary called him and Jacko knew she was right. Tom had joined as a boy and the army was mother and father to him in a way. Jacko knew that he didn't look forward to leave. He was only completely at home on the barrack square or in the Sergeants' Mess.

Tom Gilby never questioned the army, nor the orders he was given. There were times when he knew that the orders didn't make much sense but as far as he was concerned he wasn't there to have an opinion. He was there to do a job and he did it well.

Across the square the sunlight dappled through the trees lining the perimeter fence. The colour-sergeant shifted a little impatiently. It was time Major Taylor stopped and let the parade go.

The transport was already lined up by the guardroom and the men were anxious to get away and forget the army for a couple of weeks. Jacko shook his head. He knew how impossible it was going to be to forget it. People wouldn't let you. In Civvy Street they had all the answers and couldn't see why the army hadn't sorted things years back. It didn't help to try to explain and he'd long since given up trying. At least Jacko and Tom Gilby were agreed on this.

Mary didn't trust the sergeant-major. His pale face and cold eyes seemed to her to lack any sort of humour. It was as if he'd forgotten how to laugh. 'If he ever knew,' she used to say. But Jacko knew what he was and didn't give a damn. Gilby looked after Mr Thomas Gilby, and sod the world. Well, it was like that, Jacko thought. He wasn't so very different, after all, which may have been why they got on.

The colour-sergeant was a tall man. He'd been in the army since leaving school and it was the only life he knew. He'd worked his way through Junior Leaders regiment and chosen to join the Wessex Rangers because their men came mainly from his own area. There was still a tradition, even in the amalgamated regiment, and very often fathers were followed by sons into the regiment. It was dying out steadily and Jacko thought it was a pity, though his own father hadn't been in the army since '46. 'Seen enough of khaki to last my lifetime,' he used to say bitterly. 'He'd've hated Ireland,' Jacko thought. 'Not knowing who was enemy and who was friend.' At least in the Second World War it'd been clear enough who was fighting who. In Northern Ireland Jacko very often had to think twice before he knew who the enemy was and then it was simple. They were all potential enemy. The kids on the street, the women leaning out of the tenement windows, the men in the dole queues and on the street corners, the youths in the clubs and pubs and boozers were all capable of carrying a pistol or a cassette bomb and were all agreed that the British army was an institution to hate. Jacko shivered as a cloud passed across the sun. You trusted no one and that way you stayed alive, he thought cynically.

Major Taylor didn't seem to have much of a sense of humour. Certainly not one that the colour-sergeant had found whenever his recce section had been attached to B Company in the last eighteen months in Ireland. He was a cold man, Jacko felt, at the end of his time. A man with a rigid mind; good enough at the administration, but a cold fish.

Jacko couldn't say he liked him. The army had changed since Major Taylor had joined and he hadn't adapted easily to the changes. The formal divisions along social grounds were still there but partly as a result of the Irish experience the divisions of rank had come to mean much less. It was to some extent, Jacko reflected, because the men on the ground making the day-to-day contacts with the people were the junior NCOs, junior officers and men. They carried the brunt of the struggle and even an officer as hidebound in convention as Major Taylor had to recognize that.

Jacko watched as the CO's dog wandered across the front of B Company. He watched the eyes of the front rank as they followed the red setter. It stopped near Company Sergeant-Major Gilby and Jackson knew what the men were hoping. Before the dog could make up its mind the sergeant twitched his swagger cane and clipped the dog's nose. Jacko smiled. Tom Gilby hadn't appeared to move a muscle. The dog shied away and turned to amble back the way it'd come.

'I will expect to see you all on parade Monday 21st at 14:00 hours. Enjoy your leave. Sergeant-Major.'

Major Taylor had finished at last and the two men exchanged salutes. The sergeant-major turned to face B Company.

'B Company. Company . . . attention!' The crash of synchronized feet sent the red setter scuttling for cover. The men were laughing and Jacko grinned too. 'Company . . . dismiss!'

The men raced from the square past the colour-sergeant. The men of Six Platoon were as anxious as all the rest to get into civvies and onto the transport. Private Twiss nodded to the colour-sergeant as he passed him. Terry Adams walked quickly past with Privates Gadd and Mayhoe.

'Adams.' The colour-sergeant stopped the young soldier. 'Colour?'

'Going home?' asked Jackson. He liked the lad and he'd done well in his time in Recce Platoon. He had a natural ability and he, like the colour-sergeant, preferred to lie for hours watching a suspect to patrolling the squalid back streets of the little farming community they had been based in.

'Yes, Colour,' Adam replied. He wanted to get away and back to his wife. She hadn't been with them in Ireland and he wanted to see her. He wanted to forget, too, the wet street where the car had been and the memory of those faces watching and smiling as they turned away from the barricades at the end of the street. Tsai would help him forget all that. 'Yes, Colour, going home.'

Jacko nodded and the soldier moved on and rejoined his mates. Colour-Sergeant Jackson felt as glad as they all did to be off out of it.

8

Company Sergeant-Major Gilby walked slowly across to the edge of the parade ground. He smiled thinly and nodded at the departing men.

'Can't wait, can they?' he said. 'Sweetest word they ever heard, 'leave'.' he went on. He sounded almost bitter as if their rushing figures were a reproach to him and to the army. The two men walked slowly together across the square. 'Mary gone, has she?'

Tom Gilby didn't believe in wives. Women and the army - oil and bloody water, in his opinion. He'd got his share and never found anything to beat the satisfaction of running a good company, doing a soldier's job. Gilby smiled at the thought. Married to the army, people said about him and he knew it. But he didn't care, didn't feel he'd missed anything. Still, it seemed to suit some; Jacko for one.

Gilby thought he'd never understand women. He didn't really want to go on leave. He'd've been happy enough to stay on camp but the Sergeants' Mess was shutting up shop and anyway it didn't do to stay.

'She's with her mum and dad, with the kids,' Jackson said and Gilby nodded.

He'd never understood how Jacko had made it with Mary. It was about the time he'd first come across the young corporal. He'd thought then he was a pushy young bastard, but to try and make it with the girl who was teaching in the services' school in Dhekelia had seemed to Gilby, who was a sergeant at the time, to be stupid. He wouldn't stand the chance of a snowball in hell against all the young subalterns who'd be chasing her. They hadn't got much else to do in Cyprus at that time. What chance would a buckshee corporal have against the smooth young officers with their flash motors and their cut-glass voices? He'd been wrong. He looked across at the colour-sergeant walking beside him. He supposed he'd be attractive to a woman in a dark, broody sort of way. He'd obviously been

9

attractive to Mary because Jacko had worked it somehow and married her within the year. Gilby and Jackson walked together in silence as the square finally emptied of B Company.

Mary, Gilby thought, is going to be chuffed to hell when she hears the news Jacko'll take back. She's an ambitious woman and pushy for promotion. He liked her, in a way, but he knew damned well that she didn't trust him, that she could read him like a book. He knew that just as surely as he knew if he gave Jacko half a chance he'd find himself jumping to Jacko's tune. Still, he'd asked Major Taylor for him and he knew that Six Platoon wouldn't find the going as easy as they had recently.

Across the square the squat shadows of the barrack block lay over the lawns. Men were already racing down the stairs and along the balcony in their hurry to get away home. For a moment Gilby envied them. Not much longer now, he thought. Another year with B Company and then a base rat the rest of my time. Pushing a pen in some stores or doing admin, in some poxy office wasn't Tom Gilby's idea of soldiering.

'You doing anything much?' Jackson said. Leave was the end of a dark tunnel after Ireland. No restrictions, as much booze as you wanted, no chance of the bird you were taking but walking you home to a party with a Kalashnikov. Jackson looked at Tom Gilby as he stopped on the edge of the square, his cold, hard eyes staring across the grey concrete. 'Going away, get the bile out of my mouth,' said Gilby. 'Bloody Tompkins.' It'd been a quiet tour and Sergeant-Major Gilby had been looking forward to going home without a serious incident. They'd worked the usual routine of the security forces in Northern Ireland.

Their main headquarters were in a large, old RAF camp. The quarters and the mess arrangements were in prefabricated buildings or in the wooden huts strung

10

around the landing-strip. Like all RAF stations it was bleak. The open areas necessary for planes to land were a funnel for the cold and damp winds that swept down off the coast. As often as not the sky lowered over the hills in the distance and great flocks of marsh birds made their noisy nightly return to the damp river meadows beyond the old airstrip. Stranmoore Camp was a lonely place.

Married quarters were provided for all those families who chose to come. The Wessex Rangers were proud that most wives elected to accompany their husbands. If anything good could be said to have come from their garrison tour, it was the re-emergence of the family feeling of the regiment that had not been evident since the amalgamations of some years back. A new tradition building on the old. To ensure safety for the wives and the children it was necessary to split the duties of the men into external security and guards on the camp and married quarters. Each platoon spent three or four weeks in the smaller locations in the country towns and then moved back for a week of guards in the camp. While the role itself wasn't arduous, the strains and tensions of the situation were considerable for all concerned.

The Wessex Rangers had done what they could. They'd found some small arms, a cache of ammunition and a few Armalites. They'd controlled crowds at meetings and peace marches. They'd manned road blocks and sent out street patrols. They'd talked to a thousand and one people in a 'hearts and minds' operation. They'd snatched a number of known sympathizers and handed them to Intelligence for the four hours they could be questioned without being charged. They'd done well enough. Their territory had been quiet for the time they were responsible for it. They hadn't even had a man wounded until Tompkins played the hero.

Gilby's mouth tightened at the thought. That lad made him sick. They'd all had enough warning about slacking

11

off during the last few weeks of their tour. Company Sergeant-Major Gilby took it as a personal affront. One of his company spoiled the record.

'Everyone's days-to-do happy,' he'd said bitterly to Jacko at Stranmoore when they'd had a last drink in the Sergeants' Mess. 'Glad to get the taste out of my mouth and get off out of it.'

Even when it happened Tom Gilby had stared for a few moments at the wreckage of the car and then turned away bitterly. 'Dead heroes,' he'd said. 'Worse than bloody useless.'

Tompkins was eighteen and just out of depot. They'd been lucky to find enough bits to bury.

Major Taylor waited for Gilby and Jackson to join him on the edge of the square.

'Colour-Sergeant.' Jackson stopped and saluted him.

Major Taylor liked things in line, spick and span, orderly and neat. He enjoyed the army because the chains of command were clear, the demarcations between ranks worked well, and he knew where he stood. He saw little reason to change the habits and customs of a lifetime and yet the army was changing. Things go too fast, he thought. Maybe that's what the army wants but it isn't right. Messes up the pecking order, throws everything out of line.

Tom Gilby stood to one side, not sure if Taylor wanted him around or not.

'Sir . . .?' he said.

'Wait, Sergeant-Major. Please,' smiled Taylor. He knew where he stood with Mr Gilby. The sergeant-major had a view of the army that was similar to his own, he felt. They'd never discussed it. Never had to and indeed it would hardly do to pass opinions like that with a company sergeant-major. 'I'd like a word, Colour, in my office. Ten minutes, say?'

Jackson nodded. 'Yes, sir.'

Taylor turned away to Gilby. 'Doing anything exciting

12

this leave, Sergeant-Major?'

'Looking up some old friends, sir. That's all. Bit of a drink and a few old mates. Suits me, sir.'

Taylor nodded. 'Don't forget the training programme, Sergeant-Major Gilby. I'll be giving it some thought. Do the same if you've a minute.'

'Sir,' said Gilby. 'You fishing, sir, this time?'

Taylor nodded. He had a stretch on the Wye that hadn't been fished for eighteen months. He intended to take out the largest salmon in the river during the next fortnight. 'Ten minutes then, Colour.' They saluted him.

Major Taylor hesitated a moment and then turned and walked quickly away. The two soldiers watched him.

'What's that about, then?' asked Jackson.

Gilby shrugged. 'You'll have to find out, won't you? Ten minutes, the man said. See you in the Mess after. Mine's a pint if you're there first.' Gilby snapped about and strode quickly away across the empty square.

Colour-Sergeant Jackson had no time to get back to his quarter to change before seeing Major Taylor. He walked towards the barrack buildings as the first of the men raced back down the stairs in civvies. Jackson watched them dart towards the guardroom where the buses were lined up to take them to the station. Mary would be safe with her parents and settled in by now. She'd had enough of Ireland this time. She hated the restrictions and she hated the pointlessness of the work there. Mary was bitter, very bitter, as so many of the wives were. Jackson stopped at the end of the barrack block. He hadn't been affected by what went on there too much. Not until that lad bought it. It had been so stupid, so pointless and so . . . so undignified, dying like that. Strathfelt, Six Platoon's small location for the last eighteen months, had been quiet for weeks. They had had an easy stay and the battalion was due to go back to England in two weeks. There were the usual rumours, the usual chilly reception from some local

13

shopkeepers, but it had been quiet. Gilby didn't want any bother. Alongside the main communications console in the Operations Room was a plate covered with long butts. CSM Gilby was trying to give up the habit of a lifetime.

He was tired after his stint and his face was pale. The girl on the teleprinter was steadily working through a list of cars sighted around the town by street patrols. The teleprinter ticked out the numbers; if any were stolen or belonged to people they were watching the central computer would throw it up within seconds. Radios, microphones, telephones and all the paraphernalia of modern surveillance littered the table against the long wall of the Operations Room.

The phone rang. The main gate was calling in. Mr Gilby lifted the phone. 'Yes?' he said.

'Six Platoon, Three Section just coming in, sir.' reported the soldier on watch in the sangar overlooking the gate.

'Thanks,' said Gilby and put down the phone. He lit another cigarette.

Behind the sergeant-major was a panel on which were stuck fifty or so photographs of known terrorists or sympathizers. Each was attached to a map of the location by a ribbon which marked the last sighting in the area. Gilby eyed the faces with distaste: young girls known to be carriers for bomb makers or snipers, young men who were political activists, older men who had seen the previous struggles in the Province and who were bitter with a sense of failure or of betrayal and were the more dangerous for that.

Most of the pictures had flattened out the main features of the subjects. Like all official photographs taken while the subjects were being held for questioning they had been over-lit. But if nothing else the anger and frustration of the activists blazed out of the small shining squares that lined the wall.

14

The door opened and a soldier came in. Twiss was still in his patrol boots, camouflage jacket and trousers and was carrying his automatic rifle. He was soaked through. 'Frank's back,' he announced and laid his SLR down as he slumped into the only free chair in the Operations Room.

'You're sure?' asked Gilby,

Twiss looked up from undoing his boots and said angrily, ''Course I'm sure . . . sir, I saw him, didn't I?'

Private Twiss was a hard-nosed bastard, as ready with his fist as with his mouth. He knew the book, and played by the rules and regulations, but when it suited him to bend them he'd do it. He was a good soldier to have around in the streets and he didn't seem to give a monkey's for anyone. If he got an inch he'd take a mile and laugh in your face.

The sergeant-major got up and walked across to the photographs. In one the flashlight had faded out much of the detail but the curly, black hair, the beard and the cool eyes stared out at Gilby. Frank was a lone operator, a bomb maker and one of the best. The bomb experts hated finding one of his to deal with. He had a sophisticated mind, made sophisticated bombs, and he was clean. Never a word of proof, never the hint of a whisper from informants, never the chance of making a charge stick. Frank knew his business all right and was as clean as a biscuit.

In Aden, or Cyprus, or Malaya Frank would never have touched the ground till he hit a cell floor. Here, thought Gilby, you can know for sure and you still can't just walk in and snatch them. Even if you knew where to find them. Which was not the case with Frank. He was always on the move. Always a jump ahead. Gilby hated it. 'Too much politics in it for my liking,' he always said. 'Stuff opinions. Let's get on with the job.'

He'd been looking forward to returning to England

without a serious incident. If Frank was in their patch there was likely to be one. A warehouse, a police station, a bridge, a street . . .he'd hit them all in his time and never been near when the questions were asked. He'd always used a proxy, some poor terrified bastard told to drive a car, a tanker or a bus and put it outside the target. Or some besotted girl who thought she was doing the brave and clever thing by placing the package in a pub or a shop. The bomb maker never had to carry the can. Sergeant-Major Gilby hated the idea, hated having the man back. He wished to God that Twiss had shut his bloody eyes and seen nothing. One of those three little monkeys. Let the next lot clear the mess up.

The girl in the corner had stopped typing and was getting ready to leave. 'Goodnight, sir,' said the girl.

'Goodnight,' he said and the girl was surprised. He'd hardly spoken a civil word since he'd been there. She left.

Twiss leaned forward and turned up the heater. Already his wet clothes were beginning to steam in the fuggy room.

'Soldier.' Twiss looked up from lighting a cigarette. 'Put it out. I want to know what you saw, where, when and who confirmed it.'

Twiss sighed. 'Can't it wait for the debrief? I'm knackered, sir.' Gilby said nothing and Twiss got up from his chair.

'Show me,' said Gilby.

Twiss walked to the photograph on the wall. 'Him,' he said. 'We saw him . . . I saw him here.' He pointed to a collection of tight lanes and alleys in the back of the town. 'It was him all right, sir. Straight up.'

Twiss was scared of the sergeant-major. You could never work out which way the bastard would jump. A real prize bugger was Gilby, in his book. Then he'd surprise you by being out on some poxy night patrol and doing it all with you. In and out of the doorways, stopping anyone

16

moving, checking them, crossing dodgy street intersections, co-coordinating the cover as they went up each street. Or out on a vehicle check point in the pissing rain and standing his time in the cold and wet. He was fit all right, for an old man. He was thirty-four, maybe, Twiss reckoned, and that's old for crawling about the streets of Strathfelt after dark. Gilby waited a moment.

'It was Frank, sir. Honest to God. I had a good sight of him.'

Gilby sighed, nodded and picked up the phone. 'Wait,' he said. Twiss stood, still steaming gently as the damp rose from his clothes. Gilby nodded at a chair and then spoke into the handset. 'Sighting, sir . . . Frank. Yes, sir. Sector Four.' He looked across at Twiss. 'Private Twiss, sir. Six Platoon . . . which house, Twiss?'

'Sixteen,' said Twiss.

Gilby repeated the number into the handset. 'Debrief in ten minutes, sir?' he said. 'Right, sir. Will do.' Sergeant-Major Gilby stared at Twiss for a second or so and then walked across to the door. He opened it and called out, 'Two teas. Big ones and snap it up, Benson. Snap it up.' He shut the door and walked back to the console. Sergeant Bilinski walked in.

'You with him, Sergeant, were you?' asked Gilby.

'Nope. He was leading Three Section. We're a lance-jack short, Sergeant-Major,' said Bilinski. Gilby nodded.

'You might as well wait, Sergeant. Mr Preece wants a word.'

Bilinski raised an eyebrow. Lieutenant Preece was IC Recce Platoon. He'd lost a few of his best men to Recce Platoon, including his corporal. 'What the hell is he doing in?' asked the sergeant. Gilby just looked at him. A stupid question to ask when no one knew where the Recce Platoon was at any time and no one wanted to know. Not under any circumstances.

The door of the Operations Room opened and

Lieutenant Preece walked in. Gilby straightened himself and stubbed out his cigarette. Twiss slowly began to get out of his chair.

'Stay where you are, Twiss,' said Mr Preece. He was young, fresh faced, a quiet and apparently soft man. He led Recce Platoon and led it well. He'd rather spend night after night in a wet ditch watching a house, checking a suspect, watching a road, observing a bridge, than propping up the bar in the Mess. He was at home in the country and loved nothing more than being out with his men. He'd once described the character of a member of recce section as having the skills of a poacher and the morals of a sewer rat. He fitted the bill. 'You'd better tell us, Twiss,' he said, and perched on the edge of a table. A soldier brought in mugs of tea. Preece waved away the one that he was offered. 'Give it to Twiss,' he said.

Twiss took a swig. 'We'd done the street patrol to the top of Sector Six, sir. Our task, sir. I thought we'd time in hand and we'd had nothing there. The usual glad hand from anyone we saw. We were coming back across the top of Sector Four, Littlewood Street, sir. You know where I mean, sir?' Preece nodded. Mean streets, those, with half the windows bricked up and some roofs already gone where a bomb had hit. It wasn't a good place for a patrol to be and they made a point of moving through the area with great caution. Even the kids there viewed the soldiers with suspicion.

'There were three milk bottles outside number sixteen. Last time I was past there were two, and the time before that. So I dropped off the patrol and watched the house.'

'With what cover?' asked Lieutenant Preece.

'Johnny, Johnny Mayhoe. He watched me back, sir.' Preece nodded. Twiss was beginning to enjoy himself. 'I was there about twenty minutes, sir. Tucked up by the service road down the back of the new buildings. No one on the street, pissing wet, you see, sir.'

'Yes,' said Preece. 'I had noticed.'

Sarcy bastard, thought Twiss. So he got wet once in a while. He chose it, not me. 'No one to bother us, sir,' he went on. 'He moved a curtain. Upstairs. Just the once. I clocked him. It's Frank all right.'

Gilby swore softly and lit another cigarette. Preece smiled and nodded. 'Thank you, Twiss. You'd both better get into the debrief room. Then get some kip.'

Twiss and Bilinski walked to the door. Twiss stopped a moment and turned back. 'You know what I'd like to do, sir?' Preece looked around at him. 'I'd like to have him up a dark alley with the business end of this.' He held up his rifle. 'That's all it needs. Wipe the bastard off the streets.'

Preece didn't move. Gilby waited a beat and then said, 'On your way, soldier,' and Twiss walked out.

Preece walked across to look at the map. Neither he nor Gilby said anything for a moment.

'Sorry about that, sir,' said Gilby.

'Really?' asked the lieutenant. 'I know what he means. He's angry. Isn't he?' Gilby nodded.

'I had rather hoped Frank would stay out of our patch. No sightings for months and now.'

Preece shrugged. 'Now we've got to find him, I suppose. And watch him.'

Gilby sat down. 'Some were saying he'd gone for more training, sir. That's what we heard.'

Preece smiled. 'I rather hope not. He's a clever enough bastard without that, don't you think, Sergeant-Major?' Mr Preece left the Operations Room as the phone began to ring.

Chapter Two

Major Taylor's parting words on dismissing the men for their leave had annoyed Twiss. 'Have a good leave . . . delighted with the work, the backup you gave me. Regiment can be proud of you.' Bugger him,' said Twiss. 'Tell that to Gaddy.'

He sat on his bed and pulled off his shirt. Tidworth Barracks were all right. Four men to a room, lockers, shelves, hi-fi, pictures on the walls, big windows and plenty of light. A contrast to what Six Platoon had had in Strathfelt. At least here they could kip in peace, keep clean and feel like human beings again.

Across the room Adams was sitting staring at the wall. Mayhoe was already stripped and sorting out his civvy gear. The other bed wasn't occupied. Gaddy was in hospital, poor bastard, with a busted leg. Twiss thumped the bedside locker with his fist in frustration and anger. 'That bloody bomber!'

'He's all right. He's alive,' said Mayhoe. 'Surrounded by nurses and only a broken leg. I'd not give much for their chances when he gets walking again!'

'All you black sambos think about is getting a leg over, right?' said Twiss. For a moment Johnny Mayhoe stopped grinning. He'd got used to being called Jomo or Sambo. It wasn't worth getting bothered about. If any other bastard called him that they'd get done. In here, in this room, it was OK. And Twiss wasn't worth mixing it with, anyway. He was hard and punchy, and what was the point of getting on a charge for getting stuck into him? Mayhoe knew too that if Twiss was up a dark alley in Ireland he'd be as glad to have him behind him as any other soldier, black or white, in the battalion.

'Maybe,' he said. 'Maybe.' He went on dressing.

Twiss began to laugh. 'What's so funny?' asked Mayhoe.

'Gaddy. Just his luck to get male nurses.' Twiss got up and began to strip off. 'Screw his luck. You going home?'

'Yep,' said Mayhoe and pulled on his best shirt. He'd had a couple made in Cyprus when they were there. Really special shirts and some trousers too. He liked to dress well, did Johnny Mayhoe. His girl liked him to look as little like a soldier as possible. She didn't really like him being in the army. He knew it. She'd never said so but he knew it.

Twiss was pulling clothes out of his locker. He'd got over his anger. 'I'm going back home, down the pub, see a few mates, a party the birds . . . Just let us get into that suit? I got a fantastic suit, Johnny . . . Look at that!' He pulled out a dark blue three-piece suit. It was sharp, too sharp, but it'd suit Twiss and they all knew that whatever they wore didn't disguise the fact that they were soldiers. But it'd pull the birds all right. That and the money he'd saved during the eighteen months in Ireland. I'll be fighting them off.'

'Maybe,' said Mayhoe.

Twiss turned and moved over to him fast. 'What d'you mean, maybe? No bother, Jomo. You see.' He patted Mayhoe's face. Mayhoe slapped the hand away and for a moment; they stood face to face, ready to go. Johnny knew what Twiss felt about him. He knew too that he didn't give a toss for Twiss but that he wasn't going to mess up a leave for the pleasure of belting him. He grinned, and Twiss smiled touch and walked back to his bed. Twiss was worried. Going back home was no guarantee he'd see anybody. His mates were married off, or with another mob. They'd always steered clear since he joined the army. Thought he was a freak and kept well away from him. In fact the last two leaves had been bastards. A couple of drinks, maybe, and then . . . 'Sorry, mate . . . be seeing you . . . got this bit of totty waiting . . . No, she hasn't got a friend . . . sorry. You can pull your own, can't you? Put the

21

uniform on, see what happens.' Twiss knew what happened, because he'd tried it the first time he went home. They didn't want to know.

Still, it was no use telling his mates that. Leave was for having a good time, as far as they were concerned, Twiss would have had the best time anyone ever had. Ten pints a night and birds by the score. He looked across at Adams, who hadn't moved since they got into the barrack room from the square. 'What about you, Terry?' he asked Adams. 'You going home?'

Adams didn't look up.

' 'Course he's going home. Got a warm bed to get into. He's laughing, man,' said Mayhoe.

'I'll be OK.' Adams began to undo his shirt. He didn't want to go home. He just wanted to see Tsai and forget it. He didn't want to talk about it, not to Twiss nor Mayhoe nor anyone. He just wanted to get his wife out of his mum and dad's house and piss off out of it. Forget it all.

'What's the matter with you? You sound as if you'd lost a quid and found a tanner. What's the matter?' Twiss came across and stood looking down at him. Adams knew that if Twiss got the truth he'd never let it go, never stop pushing, never stop mocking. Stuff him, Adams thought. If I'd got a quarter, it'd be OK. Tsai and me . . . I wouldn't have to live in this, stuck with them all the bloody time, yakking on about the women, the booze and the good times they've never really had.

'Ball and chain, mate, a wife. No use to a soldier. You should've seen her coming and ducked out. Screw her, sure, but don't marry the bint.'

Adams looked up at the mocking face. 'I'm all right. We're going to have a ball.'

Twiss laughed. 'I should bloody hope so. Hardly seen her for months. I dunno how you stick it.' Twiss walked across and grabbed Tsai's photograph from Terry Adams's locker and chucked it to Mayhoe. Adams was on his feet fast and across for the photograph. Mayhoe held it out to him, whipped it away and chucked it back to Twiss. The two played pig-in-the-middle until Adams just stopped and sat down on the bed. The game wasn't worth playing.

'I didn't want her in Ireland. It's not right. Not for a woman,' he said quietly.

'It was all right for the others. Everyone's went except yours,' said Twiss.

'She's not one of the others, is she? My business . . . and hers. OK?'

Twiss shrugged and turned to look at himself in the mirror on the back of the door. 'Look at that suit. Knock out,' he said. Adams said nothing.

'You still on about that soldier?' asked Mayhoe quietly. Adams looked up at him and nodded.

'Not your fault, man. You couldn't stop him. No way. His fault, Terry. Nothing to do with you.'

Adams had been beside Tompkins when they found that bomb. They'd done the house-to-house together. They'd found the old woman together. And then the stupid bastard took off. Sod Tompkins. What a bitch!

At the same time elsewhere on Tidworth Barracks, Major Taylor put down the phone and checked that his fishing rods, were still in the corner of the company office. Two weeks of uninterrupted sport on the Wye would wash away the taste of the last tour. It was all part and parcel of soldiering, perhaps, but Major Taylor always found a tour in Northern Ireland depressing. Neither war nor peace, and your chaps stuck in the middle. He'd seen service all over the world and had come into the army with ambition. Now it was blunted. Maybe the next tour in Germany would see him back in Civvy Street. He wasn't looking forward to that either.

So much had changed since he'd joined up, not only in the army, but outside too. Major Taylor suddenly felt old -

too old. He sat back in his chair and picked up the file lying on his desk, Colour-Sergeant Jackson's records, papers, commendations, and service reports.

Jackson was a good soldier. He'd come in as a Junior Leader and had shown ability. He led men well and had a commendation from that Aden business. Major Taylor threw the paper back onto his desk. Reports and commendations don't make a platoon commander. There was a natural order, an order that had been honed and refined through hundreds of years of tradition and use. Platoon commanders were young commissioned officers and not NCOs, even senior NCOs like Colour-Sergeant Jackson.

Platoon command was the first responsibility of a young officer and they all understood it. The men understood, the NCOs understood. It didn't do to change things. Maybe, as the CO had said, they were short of young officers. Maybe they weren't coming forward, but it didn't make it any easier to accept the notion that Six Platoon might well be commanded by a colour-sergeant. Apart from that, Taylor could smell ambition even when it didn't directly threaten him. Jackson was ambitious all right, almost as ambitious as his wife. A knock at the door stopped Major Taylor ruminating. 'Come,' he snapped and the door opened. Colour-Sergeant Jackson stepped into the room, saluted and stood stiffly to attention. Jacko was six foot one, dark and fit. He had the habit of many physically hard men of appearing to stand on the balls of his feet. He seemed taller than he was. He'd achieved whatever he'd achieved through his own drive and talent and he was proud of that. Just as he was stubborn. Nothing would shift Jacko if he had made his mind up. He could be as tricky and devious as the next man in getting what he wanted. He'd often surprised men who had miscalculated when he was younger and he'd quite ruthlessly booted them to one side. He had ambition — Major Taylor was right enough

24

there — and his ambition was fed in part by the need to prove to Mary, his wife, that he was a worthwhile man. Her parents hadn't exactly opposed them, but he knew what they'd thought. Marrying a corporal in the infantry wasn't Mr and Mrs Barker's idea of the ideal marriage for their daughter, a teacher, well bred, well educated . . . They'd been together now for twelve years and they'd stick. But Jacko had to prove to himself that she'd been right.

'Stand at ease.' Major Taylor leaned forward to flick imaginary dust from the file before him. He picked up the pale green folder and studied it for a moment. He then laid it back on the desk and leaned back. 'CO has to see the brigadier, Colour. He asked me to have a word.'

'Sir?' Colour-Sergeant Jackson had been attached to B Company during the last few months in Ireland. He'd worked with Captain Simmons on B Company 2nd IC and had enjoyed that. He wasn't so sure about Major Taylor. Mary wasn't sure about him either, and she was a good barometer.

'Watch him, Jacko,' she'd warned. 'He doesn't like thrusters.' Jackson smiled.

'In a word, Colour, Six Platoon.'

'Sir,' said Jackson. He waited, unsure yet what the major was going to say. Outside the office he could hear men running across the road. He was as anxious as anyone to get away to his leave. Maybe the armed truce at his parents-in-law would have eased a bit by now and anyway it'd be good to put his feet up and relax for a bit.

'They're a difficult bunch.' Taylor wanted to minimize the elation he could see in the colour-sergeant's face.

'I don't know, sir.'

'I do,' replied the major. 'They're yours.'

'Sir?' asked Jackson. He still wasn't sure. The abruptness of the major's remark confused him.

25

'The platoon is yours. Your command. If you want it.'

'Yes, sir,' said Jackson. He managed to keep his face straight. A command. His own platoon. Not bad for a gash soldier, he thought. A step in the right direction, at least. Let Mary's mum and dad shove that in their pipes and smoke it.

'You don't sound too sure, Colour.' Taylor was enjoying himself. 'Didn't you want to join B Company? Have a command?'

'I'm surprised, sir. That's all. Very pleased. Thank you, sir.'

Taylor nodded. 'Don't thank me. Thank the CO. He thought you'd like to know before you go off on leave. It won't be easy.'

'Sir?'

'A temporary command is never easy, Colour.' Taylor saw the disappointment in Jackson's eyes. You know the game. A new young officer comes in . . . He'd have to take over. You must be clear about that.'

'Sir.' Jackson waited.

Taylor stood up and walked round the desk. He was anxious to get away now. 'You'll do yourself no harm. You know some of the men, I think. Adams has already settled into Six Platoon. All right?'

Jackson nodded. 'Does Sergeant-Major Gilby know, sir? About the command? Six Platoon?'

Taylor smiled. 'Company sergeant-majors have a habit of knowing before God. Haven't you noticed?' Jackson allowed a smile. Tact, Colour. That's the main thing. Tact. I'll see you after your leave to brief you.' Taylor hesitated and put out a hand. 'Delighted to have you in B Company, Colour. You'll do well.' They shook hands and Jackson saluted, turned and walked swiftly out.

Major Taylor gathered together his fishing rods and put the file away in a locker. 'I don't like it, change for the sake of it . . . never will.' He left the office door open. He

26

had one more thing to do before he took his leave. A report to write about that boy, and that'd be the last of the filth of Northern Ireland off him. Until they went back again. 'Bloody Tompkins. Bloody futile heroics. No time for it. No time.'

Part of the platoon's job in Northern Ireland was to keep an eye on suspected individuals. And it often meant long hours in the open. This particular day would have been called a soft day by an Irishman. Private Adams, lying pressed to the mushy pine needles, reckoned it was just pissing wet. Adams was right.

They'd had the house under observation for the best part of a week, day in and day out, lying under cover, dug in at the edge of the wood. The hillside sloped steeply away to a road traversing the edge of the tree line.

Recce Platoon had an OP watching the road, checking all movement in and out of the local town and across the border to the South. The road was newly made up and in the late afternoon light was shining wet. Across the valley the soft hills lay in shadow while behind Adams the pines planted by the Forestry Commission lay in black lines which allowed almost no path between each tree.

Adams shivered. The soft drizzle of the Irish morning had shaded into a downpour during the afternoon and the ground was wet and slippery. The pine needles were cold and the wet ground began to force a chill into the bones of any man who lay still for too long. The four men lay still, their blacked-up faces streaked now by the rain, their eyes strained by the constant staring through binoculars.

Eyes like bloody pandas, thought Adams. He shifted slightly and saw Colour-Sergeant Jackson look across at him. He lifted his head a fraction to reassure the sergeant and then sniffed and turned back to look away down the valley and across to the main reason for having to take up this OP.

An isolated farmhouse lay in the low pocket of ground alongside the new road. A mud track led down to the house between old broken stone walls. It had poverty written all over it. The land looked thin and arid, the few animals he'd seen were ill-kept and there was no sign of either machinery or a man about the place. It reeked of failure.

Adams shifted to take the weight on his other arm. Nothing stirred in the valley below the road. Adams was angry about the operation, angry that they were pissing wet, angry that the snatch squad had missed the bastard bomber when they went to the house where Twiss had sighted him.

They'd found a couple of detonators under the floorboards but the people there denied all knowledge of Frank. They were scared people, Adams had heard, so who could blame them? But the snatch squad should have had Frank, and would have if they hadn't ponced about waiting for someone in authority to say they could go. By the time they arrived Frank had already pushed off out of it double-quick. Now they were back to the slow grind.

Intelligence say Frank has been known to see such-and-such a man in such-and-such a club. Watch it. Watch the man. Intelligence has information that so-and-so carried for Frank at such-and-such a time. Watch them.

Intelligence could stuff itself for Terry Adams, twenty-one, married and done three of six. He'd got other problems without bothering about the Irish woman in the farmhouse across the valley who was known to be a friend, whatever that might mean, of Bomber Frank. Adams had a wife at home who wasn't happy. His parents didn't like her and didn't want her around.

He took the glasses away from his dark-rimmed eyes. He'd got enough problems without that bomb-carrying bitch. He looked back at Colour-Sergeant Jackson who was lying beside the handset three yards away across a clearing.

28

Jackson never seemed to get tired. Not dog-aching, bone-weary tired. He'd do an all-day stag and stay on when the relief party came in. Him and Lieutenant Preece seemed to like doing it. 'Takes all sorts', thought Adams, and wished he could just shut his eyes and sleep.

Private Barnard and Corporal Box lay in cover beyond Adams and were also watching. Cooper was stood down and resting - the lucky bastard. It was a simple, direct and absorbing operation and Jacko loved it. He'd rather stay out in the field than go back to the location or even Stranmoore Barracks. Recce Platoon was the best. Well disciplined, skilled and willing to chance their arm at anything. Adams was looking bushed, he thought, and crawled across the clearing to him. A good soldier, Adams, quiet, steady and a thinker. He'd do OK if he stayed in but it was time to get him a stripe or the army'd lose him.

Recce Platoon did arduous, dangerous work in exposed situations amongst hostile people. The army was on a loser in Jacko's opinion. No one liked them or trusted them. Just tools for a dirty job, he thought. Lieutenant Preece had been right. Skills of a poacher all right. As for morals, well, what morals did any bomb maker have? He didn't give a damn who got killed or maimed. He didn't really care if the carriers got an own goal and as often as not an own goal was scored in a crowded street or a shopping centre, a pub or a shop. Jacko had no time for bombers. The politics left him cold and the political activists were not his concern but bomb makers and the snipers who used kids for cover made him see red.

It was all very well to talk about community work, building a relationship with these people, but any soldier knew that at least some of these people wanted the bombing to go on, supported the makers and carriers, helped with the collections, the illegal road blocks, the terrorization of communities; any soldier felt it hard to relate to the people in the Province. The officers might manage but not the soldier, because the people he might relate to were the ones who were suffering pressure anyway. 'Stuff it all,' Jacko thought.

'I thought you liked this, Adams,' he said and grinned at the soldier. Adams wiped his arm across his face and smeared the muddy streaks already covering it.

'Sure, Colour, smashin'.' Dear mum, am sitting in an Irish bog, been here five days and four nights . . . wish you were here.' He grinned. 'When do we get relieved, Colour? I'm bloody soaked. Right through the lot.'

Jackson checked his watch. 'No idea. About an hour. With a bit of luck. I thought you'd stay.'

'In a pig's ear, Colour. I'd rather be here than on the streets, mind. You can stuff street patrols for me.'

The sun was setting behind the soft hills and it would soon be dark enough for the relief party to come and get them off the observation post.

'It's a job, Colour,' Adams went on quietly. 'Green hills, trees, birds singing, rain pissing down and that poxy bird down there not making a move. Nothing.'

She'd been out twice during the time they'd had her under observation. On both occasions she had driven through VCPs, been checked and no one had found a thing. Nothing.

'Bait,' said Jackson. 'Frank has been known to use her. Certainly to meet her. A girl friend, maybe. Bait, that's all.'

Adams sniffed. 'I hope she doesn't know it then, or we'll be stuck up here for good and all.' Jackson grinned.

'You know what Sergeant-Major Gilby calls this, Adams? Real soldiering. He'd swap us any day. He loves it.'

'He can bloody have it then, Colour. Eh?' Adams turned to look down over the darkening shadows in the valley. It was still, silent and nothing stirred by the house or along the road. A morgue.

30

The rain was sheeting down now and not one of the four men was anything but soaked through. It crept under their waterproofs and even into the tops of their boots. All for the sake of some silly, frightened, little girl, thought Jackson. He knew her face all right. He'd checked the pictures in the briefing room. She was pretty and seemed too young, too innocent, from the photograph, to be involved in bombing. These sort of people burned with fierce hatreds and prejudices that the army couldn't begin to quench. The task of the army was a holding operation, support of the RUC, low key, low profile, low intensity. The jargon of a modern engagement that involved civilians. Maybe she thinks she's doing it to save her country, thought Jackson. All I know is she's helping a bastard bomber.

'Makes me spit,' he said. Adams glanced across. 'Bomb makers. Use other people as carriers. Take no risks. Not from us anyway. We know him, we find him, watch him, but we daren't lay a premature finger on him. Wasn't that what the briefing said? 'Don't lay a premature finger. . .' Jackson laughed. 'Chance would be a fine thing. And we spend our time up to our necks in crud.'

Adams chuckled. 'You grumbling, Colour?'

'No chance, soldier. It's what the doctor ordered, is this. I'll tell you, if I see this Frank and if I get close enough there'll be an accident with my boot. He's gonna pay.'

'Have you thought, Colour - it may not be the right house? He may've gone off her. No sightings for months. He doesn't seem that keen if she is a bird of his, does he?'

'If it's not the right place I'll be spitting blood,' Jackson muttered and slithered away down into the darker shadows of the trees before standing up and walking down along the narrow track to the camouflaged Land Rover.

Adams stared down the hill, the dark camouflage on his face glistening in the rain. 'Spitting blood, Colour. You

31

just might be.'

Across the valley a light went on in the front window of the house. 'Six fifteen,' said Adams and then checked his watch. It was six fifteen on the button. She was a lady of habit, at least. Maybe Frank was too. They'd see.

Back in the control room at Strathfelt, Tom Gilby was getting on Sergeant Bilinski's nerves. The CSM was supposed to be off duty but he'd never leave it alone. It wasn't that he didn't trust anyone else to do the job, Bilinski knew that. He just didn't feel easy if he wasn't around the location or out and about the countryside. The RUC officer in the chair by the teleprinter was watching Bilinski and knew how irritated he was.

'Here, Sergeant-Major, will you not let your lads alone for five minutes, then?' the Irishman asked. Gilby stopped pacing around the room and looked puzzled. 'You never go to sleep, you stick around here day in, day out. What for, for Chrissake? It'll run itself, this. Clockwork, and nothing much on anyways.'

Gilby shrugged. He sat on the edge of a table, picked up Bilinski's cigarettes and took one.

'Help yourself,' said Bilinski and chucked him a box of matches. 'He's been giving them up the last month,' Bilinski told the RUC officer. 'Just smoking OPs now. It's the easy way to stop, yes, sir?'

The evening was relaxed enough. They had a night patrol out and about in the town and apart from that the recce platoon had their OP out in the country, Gilby was on edge. He'd rather be in the street on patrol or lying in the dark watching for that bird to make a move.

Gilby stood up. 'I'll just take a look around,' he said and walked out. Bilinski shook his head and grinned at the RUC man. 'Bloody hell, you'd think the place wouldn't run without him. There's Major Taylor got his head down in a bunk somewhere, Lieutenant James is doing a debrief, we're on in here. He could go and get his head down but he won't. Silly bugger.'

In the room behind the Operations Room a group of soldiers were watching television, playing darts or drinking tea. Company orders were that the men could have no more than two pints of beer a day. Most of the men didn't even drink that.

Gilby looked around the room. The far wall was window-less and newly built since the location had been hit by an anti-tank round some six months before. Along the wall were ranged café tables covered with slops, ash and dead mugs of cold tea. In the battered armchairs ranged in front of the television some of the soldiers slept. Gilby sucked his teeth. They were sending kids of eighteen, and after a month in the location they became hardened to lack of sleep and grabbed it where they could. Their faces were pale from tiredness and strain. It was always amazing to Gilby that their cynical humour still raised a laugh. The jokes about the Provisionals or the Loyalists or the RUC were usually obscene and always bitter. This was their closed shop and Gilby felt at home in it.

He helped himself to a mug of tea. Twiss was sitting reading the paper and eating a steak sandwich.

'Soldier,' said Gilby quietly. 'You brought up in a pig trough, were you?'

'No, sir,' said Twiss and looked almost with surprise at the steak in his hand.

'Eat in the Mess. Not in here. You must've been told ten times, if not more, Twiss. And I want this cleared up. OK?' Twiss nodded. 'OK?' Gilby repeated.

'Yes, sir,' muttered Twiss.

Gilby smiled, cold-eyed, at Twiss and was about to move on when he had a thought. 'You going on the streets tonight, Twiss?'

'Yes, sir.'

33

'Did you get any kip?'

Twiss nodded. 'Yes, sir. Some. It's a poxy place to sleep, though, isn't it, sir?'

The rooms were overcrowded and primitive. Bunk beds in long lines down the walls and across the centre of the room, strings tied from one bed to the next at head height with towels and underclothes slung on them to dry. Khaki sleeping bags on each bunk waiting for a tired soldier to crash out in them. And the incessant noise of television downstairs and of men going out and coming in along the corridor and up the stairs. Even, every so often, the muted roar of a Pig personnel carrier out in the yard. You'd get no chance of peace and quiet or privacy for the four-week stag in a location. It was a bastard. It was the place discipline mattered most, as far as Gilby could see. He liked to make his presence felt. It helped, he thought.

They'd done the best they could with the available space. They'd painted up the rooms, found, borrowed or nicked strips of carpet for the wooden stairs, but still the rooms never looked anything but pig-awful to the sergeant-major's eyes. The men were too knackered to care when they came in off a patrol. Just to eat, watch the telly, play cards and kip was all they wanted.

The old RUC station had been gutted since the arrival of the Security Forces and the internal structure altered beyond recognition. Partitions had been put up downstairs to make new rooms for the control centre and an interrogation room. The briefing room was fitted up with a blackboard and school tables which, apart from the maps and photographs on the wall, were all the furnishing.

By the main exit from the building a group of photographs warned of the dangers from snipers and urged each soldier to check and make sure before he moved to any position during a patrol. The photographs of six local children were plastered by the door. Each child was deaf and two of them had already been arrested for cheek by

34

previous battalions when they hadn't stopped on the order to do so. Each kid now had a pass to prove he or she was deaf.

Gilby walked out into the dark yard, past the sloping sand-pit which was constantly guarded. Anyone coming in had first to stop and unload his SLR or his pistol to make sure nothing was up the spout. A precaution born of sad experience, this.

'Evening, sir.' The new lad and only a kid, thought Gilby.

'How is it going?' he asked.

'All right,' said the soldier.

'Tompkins - am I right?'

'Yes, sir. Just out of depot, sir. Two days, sir.'

'Like it here, do you?' asked the sergeant-major.

Tompkins looked like the runt of the pack. He'd probably just scraped into the battalion. He was no more than eighteen.

'Where are you from, Tompkins?' Gilby asked.

'Swindon, sir,' the lad said.

'Wanted to join us, did you?' Gilby saw the hesitation in the soldier's eyes. 'Well?' he prompted.

'Nothing else, was there, sir? That or the dole. I'd had a bit of that after school, sir. So, bugger it, I thought. I'll join up.'

Gilby nodded and stepped past the corrugated iron defences around the doorway. 'That's all it takes,' he thought. 'Unemployment or a bloody war and in they come flocking.'

It was still raining. Gilby thought of Jacko stuck on a hillside and grinned. Bet the bastard's pissed off, he thought. Serve him glad.

Gilby was restless. A week to go and no sign of Frank and nothing else going on. The regular patrols, the regular chats with the known sympathizers, but all quiet. Gilby didn't Like it. It smelt of bother, he reckoned.

35

Across the yard the glow of a butt shone near the dark outline of a Pig. Gilby walked across to the personnel carrier and found Thomas, another member of Six Platoon, leaning against the heavily armoured door of the vehicle. He looked around the perimeter of the location. Lights burned down from above the sangars overlooking the main gate. The two men in each sangar covered the main gates with their rifles. There was a feeling of permanence about the outer defences of concrete, barbed wire, corrugated iron and netting that sickened the sergeant-major. I'll see me old age in here, he thought.

Thomas grinned. 'You think so, sir?' he asked. Gilby was surprised. He had been thinking aloud again.

'Not if I can help it, Thomas, Not if I can bloody help it, sonny Jim.' He strolled away back to the shelter over the door into the main building. Tompkins straightened himself as the sergeant-major walked past.

'Relax,' said Gilby and walked on down the corridor and into the Operations Room. Bilinski was on his jack with a mug of tea. He was making a note of the last message in.

'Constabulary gone, then?' said Gilby. Bilinski grinned.

'Home to bed. Just done a twelve hour stag.'

Gilby opened the door into the recreation room. 'Twiss, get us a tea will you? Plenty of sugar.' He closed the door. 'Well?' he asked.

'Quiet,' said Bilinski. 'Very quiet.'

Gilby took another of the sergeant's cigarettes. 'Be grateful for small mercies, I suppose. Another week and we're off out. No sweat. It can stay as quiet as it likes.' Bilinski was Six Platoon sergeant. His stubby face was the face of a joker. Life was too short, he reckoned, to be serious all the time. He was twenty-six, unmarried and, as far as Gilby knew, unattached. His life was the army and the Wessex Rangers in particular. A reliable man, solid.

Apart from sport his only other interest was the army. He knew more about regimental history than the CO.

The last eighteen months out here had soured him, but Sergeant Bilinski still reckoned that anything was better than poncing around Salisbury Plain playing games with tanks and blank rounds. At least there was a job to do here.

Twiss walked in with the tea for Gilby. He put it down, glanced at the two men who watched him silently. No one said a thing as he walked out and shut the door.

'Watch him,' said Gilby and Bilinski grinned.

'He's a cunning bastard, is Twiss. Knows all the answers, knows the book and knows when to stay schtum. A bastard.'

Gilby didn't like soldiers who knew the book. The army hadn't changed that much and barrack-room lawyers he could do without. It amused Bilinski to watch the two together. When their paths crossed, which wasn't often, their similarities were so evident. Twiss was stubborn; so was Gilby. Twiss did know the book; so did Gilby. Twiss was loyal to his mates, so long as it didn't affect him. Gilby was the same.

'Need to sort him, Sergeant. Nail him up.'

Bilinski nodded and picked up the handset as a message came through.

'Two, this is seagull. Over.' In the dark wood Jackson crouched close to the damp earth beside the radio. He was surprised to hear Gilby reply. 'Six two bravo, thought you'd been stood down. Over.'

Gilby took a sip of sweet tea and leaned back in the chair.

The Operations Room was warm and dry and he imagined that Jackson was neither.

'Two, only stopping to keep the lads from getting lonely. Over.'

'Six two bravo, I have a message for Sunray Minor. Over.'

'Mr Simmons about, Sergeant?' Gilby asked. Bilinski shook his head. 'Haven't seen him,' he said.

Behind them the door opened and Captain Simmons walked in quietly.

Gilby glanced round. 'Two, your lucky day. Sunray Minor just walked in.' He handed the radio set to the officer.

'Two, this is Sunray Minor. Send sitrep. Over.'

Outside the location there was a sudden roar as two Pigs revved slowly for the off. Twiss and Gadd walked past Tompkins at the sand-pit and across to their vehicles. The rest of Six Platoon were standing around waiting for Sergeant Bilinski to come out. They were due to make some spot checks and to set up snap VCPs on the main road from the town to the border. Half the platoon were still asleep on their feet. No one slept well during a four-week stag in Strathfelt.

Chapter Three

Gadd lay back in his bed in the hospital at Tidworth Barracks and stared at the white mound of bedding over the cage that covered his leg. One bomb under a culvert and up went the Pig and him with his leg jammed under the bench seat. He hadn't had a chance. When Twiss and Mayhoe pulled him out he'd cursed and sworn but he reckoned it was better than being a bloody roman candle inside the Pig when it went up in flames.

Hospital was all right apart from not smoking and the pain and the penicillin jabs. He hated it. All his mates were going on leave today and Twiss had a bird lined up for him. Had promised him. He'd get his leave, Major Taylor promised that. But all his mates would be back with the battalion. He lay staring across the ward as the nurse made up the empty bed opposite him.

She looked round and smiled at him. Fanciable, even though she slammed penicillin in his arse every morning bright and early and did it with a smile and a practised hand. True, there was no one else in the ward at the moment and there had been opportunities. But Gaddy was scared of her. He'd relied on Twiss to get him a bird for this leave and it'd always been like that. He shut his eyes. If Twiss could see him now, if Twiss could only know how he couldn't nail a bird on his own, Twiss would crucify him. He'd never let it go, the bastard. It was best to keep on the right side of Twiss or he'd make any excuse to sort you. He'd do it to anyone. Even that kid Tompkins got it while he was around.

'All right?' the girl asked as she plumped up his pillows. She smiled at him and he nodded up at her.

'You haven't got a smoke, have you?' he asked.

'No,' she said. 'And if Sister catches you again you'll

be for the high jump. Don't.'

Outside in the corridor the sound of voices raised in argument caught their attention and then Twiss and Mayhoe came in through the double doors, both of them in civvies and carrying bundles of magazines and books.

The nurse moved quickly to bar their way.

'Hang on, darling,' said Twiss. 'We had a word. We're going on leave in half an hour. Got trains to catch. Just wanted to see the wounded hero here before we went.' The nurse didn't believe him. 'Ask Sister. We told her, she said yes. Straight up, love.' She nodded.

'Five minutes, then. Doctor begins his rounds soon. Five minutes.' She bustled away. Twiss and Mayhoe watched her go, admiringly.

'You're doing all right, mate. Going to be OK,' said Mayhoe without turning to look at Gadd in his bed.

'All right!' moaned Gadd. I'm not allowed to smoke, I can't move and you lot going on leave. Sod my old mother.' The two soldiers laughed.

'I wouldn't grumble, slug. Her tuckin' you up every night. Mind yourself, mate.'

'Give up,' said Gadd. 'I was looking forward to that bird. The one you sorted.'

'Shouldn't have bust your leg then, should you? No use to you and no use to Maureen. You should see her.' Twiss stroked a body in the air. 'Join the army, Gaddy, and break a leg. Now Johnny and me, we've got a fortnight of booze and birds and no sweat. How about that?'

Mayhoe put a hand on Gadd's forehead mockingly. 'He's breaking out. You'll excite him, man. Remember what that Sister said . . . ?' Gadd struggled to sit up. 'You come here to see me or have a laugh?' he said. Twiss was enjoying it. Gadd was a lazy bastard and never lifted a finger if he could get someone to lift one for him. Twiss hadn't set up any bird for him and he was relieved that he didn't have to invent any excuses when they were on leave together. That bomber had done Twiss a favour. He looked at his watch. 'Come on, Johnny. Train.' He dumped the magazines on the bed. 'Sorry we can't stop, mate. Have a read of them.'

'Listen!' said Gadd. 'You got a smoke? She won't let us have one.' Twiss shook his head. 'No chance, mate. Rules and regulations. You should know better, Gaddy. You smoke and your leg won't get better. Tarrah then.'

Gadd watched the two young men swagger past the nurse who was at her desk at the end of the room.

'Pigs,' he said and reached for the magazines. A packet of twenty dropped from the pile. Gadd looked across at the nurse but she was checking reports as he grabbed the smokes and shoved them under his pillow.

He lay back, sweating with the effort. His leg was going to take a long time and he felt very tired.

Now that most of the men had left for their leave, the Sergeants' Mess was quiet. The bright sunlight streamed through the long windows that looked out onto a concrete patio and the pathetic attempts at a flower garden beyond. Half the officers' dogs in the camp fouled up that patch of earth and nothing Billy Harroway, the mess sergeant, could do would keep them away.

There'd been talk at one stage of trip wires and shotguns wired up, but someone pointed out that the CO might get a little niggled if his dog got splattered with shot. Billy Harroway nursed dark thoughts about all dogs, however, and was waiting his chance to sort the problem once and for all.

Around the bar, shields of other Regiments made a bright show and silver tankards gleamed on the shelves.

Tom Gilby walked through the bar door and found himself alone in the room except for RSM Fox.

'Pint, Tom?' asked Fox, and the orderly was already pulling one as Gilby joined the RSM. Mr Fox had been a soldier, man and boy and yet was young enough and fit enough to give the newest recruits trouble on the assault course. His spare body and tanned face were set off by the brightest blue eyes. Like ice when he was angry. Mr Fox never raised his voice but if he spoke most men jumped. Gilby wasn't sure what the trick was but RSM Fox certainly knew what made a man tick.

A group of sergeants came through, ordered their drinks and moved away to the tables on the other side of the room in the sunshine. A final bevvy before moving off camp with their wives and kids, thought Gilby.

'Get away from it. Get a perspective, Tom,' Mr Fox was saying. 'You live here all the time and you'll bleed the army.'

'I don't mind,' agreed Gilby. 'I've got a lot of friends to look up.'

He drank some beer. He hadn't a clue where he was going. He'd just get in the car and drive. A sort of refugee in alien territory. Maybe he'd go up to Catterick. There was a pub there that used to do bed and breakfast. That'd suit, Gilby thought. Two weeks to kill before we get back. Get a drink in of an evening, have a chat. There's bound to be someone I know up there. The Bedfords are based there. Gilby had checked. He'd have some old mates to chat to, some soldiers to talk with. He might even pay their mess a visit. It'd take care of a couple of nights anyway. And he'd be bound to find someone who had been in Hong Kong, or Aden, or Cyprus when he was there. Maybe it wouldn't be so bad after all.

'You got the man you wanted. You should be happy,' said Mr Fox as Gilby supped up the last of his pint. 'Jackson'll make that platoon work. It's what they need.'

'Agreed.'

'Just so long as you know it was discussed, Tom. I'll have the same again. Ta.'

Gilby got the round in. Sure, they talked about it. Will

Tom Gilby wet his knickers having a senior NCO in command of a platoon? A subaltern wet behind the ears is one thing, but a man with time in is something else. Discussed it, bull. They just organized it. It screws up the shape. A raw subaltern was meat and drink to any CSM worth his salt. The good ones you help; the bad ones, well, it was up to them.

'Cheers,' said Gilby and smiled as Mr Fox drank his pint. 'Seeing some old mates, then?' said Mr Fox.

'Well,' said Gilby, 'to tell the truth, and just between us, I know someone who's, well, widowed like. See?' He tapped the side of his nose and winked.

'Dark horse,' said RSM Fox, who didn't believe a word of it. Tom Gilby grinned. 'Only young, mind. And always glad to see me.'

'She'll nail you down, Tom. Watch yourself. She'll nail you. And my wife would be chuffed as little apples.'

Gilby shook his head. 'Not me, sir. Not me.'

The RSM checked the time on the bar clock, drank off his pint. 'Sorry, Tom, my wife'll skin me. Have a good leave,' he said and hurried away. Gilby turned from the bar and looked around the room. The group in the corner was larger and it looked like becoming a party. There was a lot of laughter and shouting. Like kids out of school, thought Gilby.

It all gets washed away and forgotten till the next time and next time we'll get someone else with a bullet up his arse, or kneecapped or bombed or shot at with Russian anti-tank rounds or whatever delight they've dreamed up by then.

Gilby ordered another pint. He had seen men shot, others with shrapnel in their groins, others, plenty of them, wounded and screaming for help. When he'd been a youngster he'd not bothered too much. You joined up, you were trained and you expected to get the same one day. You could so easily be soft that you automatically built a

43

shell around you. You'd walk out of something where you'd lost a mate and in a couple of days it was forgotten. Or, if not exactly forgotten, it was only a dull memory. But he couldn't get out of his mind the smoking wreckage of the car, the shattered windows in the houses around and a couple of soldiers with faces bleeding from flying glass. Above all he kept on seeing that lad standing by the sand-pit in the doorway of the location, white-faced, new and very serious. Afraid, if he could think at all, and not yet secure in the knowledge of the expertise surrounding him. Gilby couldn't get Tompkins's face out of his mind.

On the hillside the rain had eased off a little. The OP section still lay watching the road and the farm through night glasses. If anyone was going to make a contact it would be around this time. The light downstairs was still gleaming and even from this distance Adams could make out the shape of a couple of plant pots on the window sill. Nothing grew in them. Behind him Adams felt rather than heard Colour-Sergeant Jackson as he eased into position. No sign of relief section, thought Adams. The bastards are late again. Jackson crawled alongside him.

'Anything?' he asked. Adams handed him the night glasses without a word. Jacko looked once and handed them back.

Adams was grinning.

'What's so bloody funny, then?' asked Jackson.

'Us,' said Adams, and the light went out downstairs in the farmhouse. Adams lay with the night glasses focused on the house. Nothing moved in the area. The night was silent except for the rain dripping off the trees behind them. After a few moments the light went on upstairs. 'There you go,' said Adams. 'Kip. Clean sheets, soft bed. Eh? I could use that, Colour, couldn't you? We're bloody mad.'

44

Jackson took the glasses and watched. The woman drew the curtains as she had every night. Nothing was going to happen tonight, he could feel it in his bones.

'Have you ever thought what you might be doing?' Jackson asked without taking his eyes off the farmhouse.

'A civvie?' said Adams. 'I wouldn't be here, would I? I'd be down the factory. Night shift now and double time as likely as not. Me dad wanted to fix it, said he could set me on.'

The rows they had had about that when he announced that he was joining the army. His dad kept on and on at him about it. His mum too. She hadn't wanted him to go into the army. It was as if he'd betrayed them in some way, as if the army was a muck heap and only for rubbish. He'd've been turning out small parts by the thousand and going barmy with it if he'd stayed.

'I'd be making a bomb, Colour.' Adams realized what he'd said. 'Sorry.'

The two men grinned. It didn't seem very real, being stuck here in the country, watching the house of a woman who was probably as nice as anyone else, who certainly was brave and might just possibly have some reason for being suspicious of the army. After all, they were 'peeping tomming' on her day in and day out. Adams wondered what his mum would feel if she was in that woman's position.

'What about you, Colour?' Adams asked.

'Never think about it. You get some time in and you stop bothering. I'm all right.'

It was true. Jacko had thought about it for years now. Most of his friends were army people; in most of the places he went he mixed with the services and didn't bother mixing too much with the locals. In Cyprus he'd hardly ever talked to a Cypriot and in Germany he didn't speak the language and not many spoke English, so what was the point? The army was his shell and he liked it.

45

Nothing outside could touch it. Where else could you do something like this? Looking for a dangerous man, making sure you eventually nailed him up and making the place safer? The rights and wrongs weren't his problem. Colour-Sergeant Jackson didn't have an opinion about the Irish problem. Not his to bother about, let the officers and the politicians have opinions if they wanted. He had a job and as far as he was concerned he was trying to sort out a mad animal. He'd do it too, if he could.

The rain had stopped and even the dripping from the pine trees was only spasmodic.

'I'd rather be here than anywhere, Adams. Not bunked up in that location. Sergeant Bilinski and Twiss and Mayhoe and all the rest - bored out of their skulls half the time and scared witless the rest.'

'Fuck that,' said Adams. 'You scared?'

Jackson didn't know. 'It's a job. Do it. Do it right. That's all about it.'

Down the hill a dog barked once. The bedroom light went out.

Not so far away, on the main road from Strathfelt to Tangannon two Pigs were placed across the road. A 'rat trap' had been ordered and anything or anyone that moved along the road was to be stopped, searched and questioned.

Most of the traffic through had been local and the people, who were used to searches by now, had been uncommunicative.

Sergeant Bilinski cradled his cold rifle and waited beside the first Pig. The radio operator was sitting in the cab and out in the darkness Bilinski knew he had cover from one man on the hill, from another in the ditch at the side of the road and from a third man near a broken stone gate. It didn't do take any chances when you stopped and searched and Sergeant Bilinski wasn't taking any.

Twiss leaned against the bonnet of the Pig and automatically checked over his SLR. Bilinski looked at his watch.

'Bloody waste of time, Sarge,' said Twiss and spat. 'Stop 'em, chat 'tem up, thank you very much for your help. Useless.' Bilinski was inclined to agree.

'You just do it, Twiss, and stop bellyaching,' said the sergeant. He'd had enough of Twiss already tonight. Three hours of wandering about the country, setting up VCPs and then moving on again. Sometimes, though, a spot check like this threw someone into the net. It was a long shot but it could just work.

'You think we're going to get that bomber by stopping cars? He'll've gone to ground. I would. I mean, he must know we've seen him, what with the search on the house and all that. I'd go to ground and I bet he has. We won't get a bloody cheep out of him, will we?'

'I hope you're right. It won't be a cheep we'll get if we do hear anything. It'll be a bloody great bang and people dead. That's his fucking mark, Twiss. All right? And it's not him we're watching for, is it? It's her. Watch her, check her movements. She'll take us to him.'

Twiss slammed the butt of his rifle against the towbar of the personnel carrier.

'In a pig's ear 'ole,' he muttered and walked out into the road as a car drove slowly towards the check point. Bilinski covered him and the two other soldiers who moved out of the shadows towards the car.

Back at base, CSM Gilby sat in the canteen and watched as the men straggled in from a street patrol. They were-wet, dirty and still had camouflage paint across their faces. He watched as Zorro Yates pushed past the new kid, Tompkins, up to the front of the queue.

' 'Ang on, 'ang on,' yelled the cook and banged a couple of hands away with a ladle. On the grill steaks sizzled and burned as the men waited. Tompkins said

47

something to Zorro, who turned round fast and was about to thump the kid.

'Yates. You, Yates. Here!' snapped Gilby from the other side of the room. Yates hesitated and then walked across to him.

'Yes, sir?' he said. His black hair was sleeked down by the rain, his camouflage jacket was wet and Gilby could see the outline of the flak jacket that Yates had dangling in his hand.

'Hungry, Yates?' Gilby asked, and Yates said nothing. Just stared ahead. 'Hungry, are you?' Gilby repeated quietly. The other soldiers were getting their food and Zorro Yates had lost his place in the queue. 'Pushy, aren't you? Manners of a pig.'

Yates still said nothing. Just stared ahead at the wall behind Gilby's left shoulder.

'That kid.' Gilby went on. 'Look at me, soldier. That kid. He's just away from his mother's tit and you put your weight on him. Big lad, aren't you?'

'Sir?' said Yates, all innocence.

More of Six Platoon clattered through the door and joined the queue. Gilby watched Yates's eyes. He wanted to get back and eat.

'Sit down, soldier.' Yates hesitated. 'Sit down!' Yates sat down. 'Now tell me what you saw.'

'The usual. Nothing. We chatted up a few who'd talk to us, sir. Didn't see a blind thing out of line like. Not a nicked car, not an extra bottle, no drawn curtains where curtains don't usually get drawn. The place is clean. Not a dicky bird, sir.'

'You say,' said Gilby. That bastard is around somewhere.' Yates shook his head. 'Don't believe it, sir. Even if he was sighted, sir. It's bloody stand-up. A false alarm.'

Gilby snapped, 'Not what Int. tells us, Yates. You know better, do you? He's on this patch somewhere.'

Yates said nothing.

'That kid. Was he scared?'

Yates shrugged. Gilby looked across the room to where Tompkins was sitting alone.

'He'd be the first who wasn't. I don't want him buggered about, Yates. Watch it.' Gilby got up and walked past the youngster. 'All right, son?' he asked and Tompkins nodded as he gulped down his steak.

The sergeant-major had been promised a lift by Major Taylor. He fancied a break, a few hours in a decent bed back at Stranmoore Barracks. Just to be fresh for the morning. He walked out of the dining room.

That night was a bastard of a night for an OP. The moon was up and any cloud cover had gone. Bloody typical thought Jacko as he approached the Land Rover. The relief party get it cushy again.'

'Evening, Colour,' said Lieutenant Preece. Jacko hadn't heard him coming.

'What's the matter, sir? Where's our relief party?' asked Jackson.

'Just tell me what's happened first, Colour. Please.' The two men got quietly into the front of the Land Rover before Jackson began his report.

'Nothing, sir,' he said, and Preece sighed.

'Waste of time then, do you think?' he asked.

Jackson wasn't sure what he wanted to hear. A week spent uselessly on an OP was part of the game, and if the bomber, Frank, had decided not to show up at his old girl friend's, well and good. It was a contact eliminated, to an extent.

'She has carried stuff, sir. She's the obvious one,' he said. They'd've looked fools if they hadn't covered her but he knew as well as Lieutenant Preece that Recce Platoon were stretched. They'd too much ground to cover and too many other OPs to man. It was all a matter of priorities.

49

'We can't afford it, Colour. A section of men tied up for B Company. They don't like it.' Jackson grinned. He knew Preece and he knew damned well what he wanted.

'Who can't afford it, sir? The company, the battalion . . . or recce section ?'

Preece thought for a moment. He stared out of the windscreen of the Land Rover into the dark trees. Nothing to be seen, nothing to be heard. Somewhere out in that night was a man making a bomb, or thinking about making one, or making sure that a bomb was put out by some poor bastard. Lieutenant Preece sniffed.

'I think we can stand down for the night. Come out early in the morning. I've had a word with Major Taylor. He'll go along with it,' he said. Jackson nodded. 'They will be glad of a break, sir,' he said.

'Not complaining, are they, Colour?' Lieutenant Preece asked.

'Not so's you'd notice, sir,' said Jackson. I'll go up and tell them.'

He got out of the Land Rover and quietly stalked away up the hill. Preece watched him for a moment and then stretched out. He was dog tired, he suddenly realized. He hadn't slept for four nights. Not properly. Even when he came into barracks after leaving a section on an OP he was never at ease. The tension only went when he was back in the field and had found that his men were all right.

Twiss was cold. He and Three Section had been checking the slow trickle of cars coming through their VCPs for ages now. All Twiss wanted was to get his head down. He'd had enough of being polite to the drivers, checking their papers, opening the boots of their cars, covering while Burroughs or Hunt or one of the others searched.

Along the road two pairs of headlights threw up dark shadows. Land Rovers, thought Twiss. Bilinski, Hunt and

Burroughs joined him on the apex of the VCP. In the darkness behind them they knew they were well covered by the rest of the section.

Twiss stepped forward with a light and slowly waved the front Land Rover down.

'Cold, Twiss?' asked Jackson, poking his head out of the second vehicle.

'On your way, sir,' said Twiss. 'It's all bloody right for some.'

The recce vehicles drove quickly through the block and away.

'Lucky bastards,' muttered Twiss. 'We come here, hands behind our backs. Eyes half-shut, blindfolded more like, by the politicos. "Be good boys. Play patsy" I don't bloody like it.'

Bilinski stopped in his tracks, turned back to Twiss and Twiss stopped.

'Finished, Twiss?' he asked. Twiss nodded. 'Stay finished,' said Bilinski and stepped away into the darkness beyond the second Pig.

For Twiss the solutions were easy and plain as the door of a Pig. These people fighting each other, setting themselves up, running road blocks, shooting and looting and maiming each other, weren't going to stop doing it because they had a soft pat on the head and got told to be good boys. Twiss was standing in the middle and he knew one thing - it was a bastard.

He leaned back against the Pig in the dark and stared into the night. Twenty, curly-haired, white-faced and eyes like slate. He'd seen enough and heard enough and he didn't talk about it all when he got home. He started to laugh. It was the first time he'd laughed since he got out here, Twiss thought. And he was laughing about Germany, not this poxy, sodding island. Gadd walked past and saw him grinning at nothing.

'What's on?' he asked. 'Grinning like a fart. What is

it?' Twiss turned to him fast, angry at being discovered.

'Nothing,' he said. 'Yeah, yeah, it was. I was in Germany, club dancing a bit and bloke comes in . . . dark it was, you know. And didn't see me behind the pillar and whop! He zapped me in the face with a glass. I fell over the back of a chair and looked up and everyone was fighting around the fuckin' place.' Twiss grinned at the memory. 'He picks us up and he says he is sorry, a mistake, some bird or other. He was fuckin' sorry . . .' Twiss grinned again and Gadd shook his head.

'All I remember about Celle was big Elsa, remember her? Tits the size of fuckin' footballs. Everyone went through her first off. Her and old Smokey . . . remember? She gave me a dose. Fuckin' cow.'

'Serve you glad. Dirty sod, going with our Elsa,' laughed Twiss.

'Twiss!' Bilinski had the light and was flagging down a car.

Company Sergeant-Major Gilby nursed a Browning on his lap as Major Taylor drove towards Stranmoore Camp. They hadn't spoken for some minutes. Gilby eased a packet of cigarettes from his pocket.

'Smoke, sir?' he asked. Major Taylor shook his head.

'You go ahead, Sergeant-Major.' he said. Gilby lit up. 'It's too quiet, Sergeant-Major. Don't like it like this. Int. thinks we're in for something. So do I.'

Gilby agreed. 'That new lad, Tompkins, sir. They're sending us kids, aren't they?'

Major Taylor smiled. It was a constant beef from Gilby, this. He seemed to think you could pluck experienced men from thin air. 'How is he?'

'All right, sir. He will be. Did a street patrol today. I don't think he enjoyed it.'

'Not sure I would, Sergeant-Major. It's hardly a bed of roses in that location. Couldn't say they exactly love us

52

down there.'

'I don't want them to love us, sir. I just want them quiet for the next few days. We will get out on schedule, I suppose?'

'We'd better, Sergeant-Major. I've promised myself a fortnight's fishing when we get back. I've a stretch of water I haven't touched for a long, long time now. You know anything about fishing?'

'Not me, sir. Bilinski does some, I think. He goes on about it. Not my sort of sport, I'm afraid.'

The car drove on through the dark lanes, past small groups of houses, overgrown farm gates, small, isolated pubs. Everywhere in darkness, without even a light showing. Gilby leaned back in the seat and checked the pistol again. No one travelled even in a civilian unmarked car without a weapon. Occasionally on this road an illegal road block had been set up, and they were sitting ducks for a terrorist patrol. As far as Gilby was concerned everyone in the Province was enemy. An old woman pushing a pram down a country lane could be carrying weapons under the baby; a bunch of school kids yelling down a street could be a decoy to take a patrol within range of a sniper in a block of flats; a girl with a shopping bag could be carrying a cassette filled with phosphorus or magnesium; the old man on the corner could be a political officer or a group organizer; the youths in the street could be spotters checking the number of your car as you drove in and out of the location. They were well organized and it didn't do to take a single chance. He'd seen service in other places and in all cases the whole population, as far as Mr Gilby was concerned, were targets. No use trying to make any exceptions, for you always got let down.

The black butt of the Browning was cool in his hand.

'Put it away, Sergeant-Major, please,' said Major Taylor. 'Those bloody things make me nervous.' He grinned across at the sergeant-major.

53

They'd been together in Aden when Gilby was a corporal and he was a lieutenant. They'd done a couple of operations together and Major Taylor knew then that Gilby had the makings of a soldier. He was hard as bullets, ruthless, demanding and no one's fool. He'd think before he took a chance and the risk was always a calculated one.

'Be glad to get out this time, Sergeant-Major?'

'Glad enough. Always glad. Mopping up job, really. Other people's bloody mess, sir. Excuse me. Makes me bitter, sir. Very.'

Major Taylor agreed. 'Those are the rules,' he said. Gilby scowled into the darkness.

'Don't I know it, sir. Last tour we lost two from the battalion. One the time before. So far we're clean, but you can't be sure, can you? Not till the last man is on the aircraft back. Never sure, are we?'

'I suppose not.'

'Don't even have a good reason for losing them, do we, sir?'

Major Taylor smiled. 'An opinion, Sergeant-Major?'

'Not supposed to have them, are we, sir? Opinions are for the others. Not for us. Luxury item in my book.' They drove on through the darkened countryside towards Londonderry.

The car Bilinski had flagged was slowing down. The woman driving wound down her window. A pretty woman with long, straight hair. She smiled up at the sergeant as he shone his light on her.

'Good evening, Sergeant.' She handed him her licence.

'Would you mind, madam?'

She shrugged and got out of the car. Twiss and Gadd stood beyond the circle of light, vague figures in the dark. Their SLR rifles were covering the car and the woman.

54

Even in the dim light they could see that she was a looker. She'd a trim figure and the dark blue eyes of some of the locals, and in any other circumstances they'd've been chatting her up without the aid of a rifle. She looked incuriously towards the two soldiers.

'Late, isn't it, Sergeant?' she asked.

'Twiss.' Bilinski nodded at the boot of the car. Twiss moved fast across to the back of the car, opened it and did a quick check. Nothing but an empty oil can, spare wheel, tool kit. Nothing for them.

He slammed the boot lid and went towards the back door of the car. He looked carefully inside and then opened the door.

'There's nothing to interest you, Sergeant,' said the woman and smiled at him again.

'Where are you going?' Sergeant Bilinski asked.

'My uncle wanted to see me. Family business,' she said. Bilinski made a note on the note pad.

'Where?' he asked.

'Just over the hill. There's a farm off the track about five miles. You know the one, Sergeant?' she asked and Bilinski nodded.

'Yes, I know it. Your uncle?'

'Yes,' she said.

Twiss slammed the door of the car and walked slowly across to the two of them. 'Nothing, Sergeant,' he said. 'Clean as a whistle.'

Bilinski smiled at the woman as he handed back her licence. Thank you, madam,' he said. 'On your way.' She got back into the car. 'Will you be coming back tonight, madam?' She shook her head. 'I haven't a clue. Sorry,' she said. 'Goodnight, Sergeant.'

The car drove away into the dark road. Bilinski moved quickly to the front Pig and reached inside for the handset.

Twiss moved with him. 'Her?' he said. Bilinski was already calling base.

'Hello, two, this is two three. Over.' He nodded at Twiss who scowled.

Twiss turned back to Hunt savagely. 'See that? That bitch. Her. Frank the bomber's bird. A fucking carrier. Known. What do we do? "Thank you, madam, please, madam, on your way, madam . . ." '

Bilinski waved an impatient hand to Twiss to shut up. 'She just drove through our position, heading in the direction of town.'

The road dipped down through, a clump of trees and ran for a time parallel with the railway track and then curved round and over a bridge. A track ran down from the road to the railway for the use of track supervisors. Under the bridge an old van was parked. It was hidden in the dark shadow of the bridge and even with the moon up it was impossible to see the van from the bridge or from the road. There was no reason for the van to be under the bridge but no one was about to ask questions and if they had been it is doubtful if anyone would have answered.

In the leading Pig, Twiss and Mayhoe were sitting on the hard benches that ran down each side of the heavily armoured vehicle. Up front Sergeant Bilinski sat with his menacing rifle poked out into the night through the slit that served as windscreen. The rear Pig was close behind them. The VCP had been called off immediately the woman went through their check point. The observation post had already come off the hillside and no one felt it necessary to continue on watch. Even if they had, they were too stretched in other areas to persist with what seemed to have become a futile check. Checks had been done and there was no doubt that the woman's uncle lived where she said. Twiss and the rest were happy enough to be taken off the check point and to drive back into camp.

'Waste of bloody time,' yelled Mayhoe over the roar of the engine. 'We could've been in our bloody pits the last hour.'

Twiss's fingers moved continuously over the SLR as he rode with the bumps and thuds of the Pig. Check the spring, check the trigger, check the clip, check and recheck and re-check again. All the time his fingers were spidering over the weapon, touching, reassuring themselves that it was still there, still efficient, still a part of the rest of his body, an extension. He sniffed, shut his eyes and leaned back against the thudding swings of the Pig.

'And if we'd found him, the bomber, you'd've been a bloody hero. Fucking amazing, innit?' he said.

The road dipped between the clump of trees and the Pig swung along the road parallel with the railway track. In the back no one said anything now. They just wanted to get some shut-eye. Mayhoe was almost asleep. Ahead of them the stone walls at the edge of the bridge gleamed wet in the headlights. The driver slowed a fraction and then roared on over the bridge.

As the second Pig hit the centre of the bridge, the van parked below blew up, screaming, jagged metal slammed into the arch and the force of the explosion blew the road up and out to catch the vehicle. The Pig tipped, raced on and then swung slowly over and thudded into the supporting wall of the bridge. The engine still roared and then suddenly stopped. Already the section in the lead Pig had hit the ground and fanned out. Bilinski yelled his instructions at the men, still slightly deafened not only by the explosion but also by the continuous roar of the Pig's engine.

'Cover on the right, Paterson, Roberts . . . Hunt, take the left and the track with Jenkins. Move yourselves!'

By the time they had deployed and were covering the road and track from all angles the back door of the toppled Pig was open and men were crossing the bridge fast towards Bilinski. He checked them as they came across.

'Camden, Hargrave, Furst, Rogers . . . where the hell is Gadd? Where is he?'

57

Mayhoe and Twiss heard him ask and were already racing across the bridge, crouched and moving fast. They had cover on both sides from the parapet of the bridge but were exposed if anyone opened up from the direction they had just come from. They reached the twisted vehicle.

'Where the hell is he?' asked Mayhoe.

'I thought you lot could see in the dark, Sambo,' said Twiss savagely. 'He'll be in the back.'

The two men got into the shambles in the back of the Pig and found Gadd lying wedged under the bench. His leg was obviously broken and he was moaning with pain.

Mayhoe and Twiss tried to clear his damaged leg without hurting him.

'Jesus wept,' yelled Gadd.

'Pull him, pull him clear before the lot goes up,' shouted Twiss and he and Mayhoe pulled. Gadd yelled once more and then passed out. The two men stumbled through the dark across the bridge, carrying Gadd between them.

As they crossed the bridge the sky lit up as the fuel in the Pig caught light. They took Gadd straight between the line of covering soldiers and past Bilinski as he stood staring at the flames from the Pig.

'Bastard bombers . . . bastards, all of them,' yelled Twiss to no one at all. There was no noise now as they covered Gadd with their jackets and laid him on the bench for the drive back to the location.

'And you,' said Twiss to the driver, 'take it fucking easy. This isn't a roller coaster. If he makes a sound I'll have your balls.'

Bilinski was already on the radio. 'Hello, two, this is two three. Over.'

At last something had broken. The bomber had made his first move. It was a start.

The men sat in the back of the Pig holding Gadd down on the seat, their faces pale in the blue light shining from the internal bulb over their heads. Twiss kept patting his gun and muttering angrily to himself. All he wanted was a half-second to sight that fucker Frank and they would be bothered by him no more. Bastard.

Chapter Four

Jackson decided to have one drink before he left to rejoin Mary and the kids at her parents. But he hesitated a moment when he saw Sergeant Bilinski and Tom Gilby talking over drinks in the Sergeants' Mess.

He wasn't sure how Bilinski would take the news that he was getting command of Six Platoon.

He did know he'd have to tread carefully and break the news at the right time. He wasn't sure how much Tom Gilby had already told the sergeant.

His pint was already pulled by the time he had crossed the room.

'Drink up, then Jacko. Congratulations,' said Gilby and raised his glass. Bilinski looked puzzled.

'What's on, then?' he asked.

Jacko cursed Gilby for a tactless bastard. He'd probably set it up deliberately.

'I've got a command,' said Jacko and hoped that Gilby would let it ride at that.

He didn't.

'Tell him which platoon, Jacko.'

Jacko leaned on the bar and looked past Tom Gilby to the dining-room door. Only one place was laid and he'd put money down it was for the company sergeant-major. Gilby'd be last out of camp when he wanted to stir the pudding a bit. Tom Gilby didn't let go.

'Tell him,' he said.

'Six,' said Jacko reluctantly. Bilinski's smile was fixed. He'd been enjoying running the platoon and he didn't want anyone else in command. He'd known, of course, that they'd eventually promote someone, but he'd assumed it'd wait until they got their next young subaltern, fresh and inexperienced from Sandhurst.

For an experienced sergeant like Bilinski that would have made life very simple. He knew the ropes, the young officer wouldn't; he knew the men, the young officer wouldn't, and if that young man had any sense he'd have left much of the routine to his sergeant; Bilinski was disappointed and it showed.

'All right, Bil?' asked Jacko. He knew what he'd feel and from the look on Bilinski's face he was feeling the same. Jacko could've zapped Gilby at that moment and the pale, smiling face vanished behind the pint glass. Bilinski shrugged and put down his pint. 'I thought, well, maybe they'd let it ride. I could've managed.'

Major Taylor had been right about the need for tact. Jacko smiled and snapped a finger at the bar steward for another round.

'I know that. We all know you could. Young officers are short. We know that too. Major Taylor made it clear it was temporary.'

'Sure,' said Bilinski and finished his drink. Gilby smiled thinly as he watched the interplay. The promotion made some problems for him and he didn't see why those problems shouldn't be shared about a bit.

'No reflection on you, Bil, is it?' the sergeant-major said. 'It's going to work out. Don't worry about it.' Jacko pushed the fresh pint along the bar to the sergeant.

'I'm not disappointed . . . well, I am really. I was looking forward . . . Still, I'd rather have you, Jacko, than some wet-eared laddie from training.'

It was hardly a compliment. 'Thanks very much,' said Jacko dryly, and Bilinski grinned from ear to ear. 'I didn't mean it like that,' he said.

It wasn't going to be easy for any of them. Jacko had to fit into the company and although that in itself wouldn't be hard in ordinary circumstances, to come in as a colour-sergeant commanding a platoon would set up changes in the pecking order for all of them. Bilinski would be seeing him every day on and off duty as they used the same mess. Gilby would be outranking him technically, and yet Jacko would have the problems and responsibilities of a commissioned officer. It wasn't going to be a bed of roses for anyone and they all knew it. They were going to have to tread carefully, one with the other, for a time. It was probably just as well that they were going on leave immediately. It'd give them time to get used to the idea.

'When are you off, Jacko? Eating first?' Gilby broke the moment's silence.

'No, Tom. I'm going up to her mum's place by train. She took the car with the kids. I'll be away in a minute or two.' Jacko had already changed into civvies. Bilinski, too, was in civvies but Tom Gilby was still in working dress. He resented changing out of it into sports jacket and casual trousers.

Jacko sank his pint and Gilby had already got the next one in. Bilinski tried to refuse but Gilby insisted.

Jacko still felt edgy after Ireland. The nerve ends still jangled with the effect of eighteen months of constant tension and he needed to unwind. He knew very well that Mary's father would be on at him the minute he arrived. Mr Barker had been a soldier in the last war and never stopped talking about how they'd dealt with the tribesmen on the Indian Frontier. He couldn't seem to see much difference between them and the Irish problem. Indeed, he had strong opinions about what the army should do and he never let it alone. Jacko knew he'd have to hold himself in check and he knew that Mary found it a strain too. Her mother would have been delighted if a crack could be found in their marriage and Jacko knew that Mary was also suffering from the strains of the past tour.

He was happy enough about her. The marriage seemed to him to be all right. He'd never actually asked Mary what she thought but she'd tell him if anything was really wrong. They had their bad patches but Jacko consoled himself that these were the normal bad patches of any marriage. The army did put a strain on any relationship and the absences in Ireland or on training didn't help. The name of the game Jacko, always said. They'd both known what it would be like and Mary had enough interests outside the army and her home to keep herself occupied. Some of the wives worked when they could find it. For some it was a necessity, but Jacko didn't really approve and Mary wouldn't find any teaching jobs for the temporary periods she was around in any quarter.

'What's up, then, Jacko?' asked Tom Gilby. 'Thinking dark thoughts?'

Jacko smiled and shook his head.

Mary had been very good with his soldiers too. She'd always kept an eye on the young wives when their husbands were in the locations and away from camp. It wasn't easy for the girls who married soldiers.

In some ways Jacko agreed with Gilby. Women and the army, oil and bloody water. The soldiers all seemed to marry too young. There was a lot to be said for the old system when a soldier had to ask permission of his commanding officer before he could marry. He smiled at the thought. If they'd worked the old system he'd never have married Mary. Forget it, he thought, and drank up.

In barrack room A, Block Four, Adams still sat on his bed. He'd changed into a leather jacket and waterproof over-trousers and had dumped his crash hat on the bed beside him. He couldn't work up the enthusiasm to get his motor bike and leave camp. Twiss and Mayhoe were just about off.

It's all right for them, Adams thought. They don't have a load of bother waiting for them when they get back home. Twiss'll dance and drink, fight and fuck his way through leave and Mayhoe'll do all right with his steady bird. He hadn't heard from Tsai for over a week now. She

63

hadn't phoned him like she used to do and she hadn't written either. She didn't find writing very easy, which wasn't surprising.

He'd had a hard time when he'd told Major Taylor he wanted to marry a local girl. They'd been on a jungle training course in Malaya and he'd met her there. She wasn't the usual good-time bird down the bars and brothels of the local town. She was quiet, subdued in a way, until she smiled. Her mother and father hadn't liked the idea, she told him, but be buggered to them. Major Taylor had warned him against it and when he'd brought her home to his mum and dad, Adams almost began to wish he'd taken his advice.

His mother hadn't said a blind word. Just looked thin-lipped and turned away into the back kitchen. Not a word of welcome, nothing, and his dad hadn't been much better. He'd hardly looked up from the racing on the telly. He'd nodded at her, grunted at him and settled back with the flickering black-and-white picture.

'You don't want to go, do you?' said Mayhoe and sat down beside Adams.

Mayhoe was the only black Terry Adams had ever talked to. Before Johnny came into the billet, he and Twiss didn't like the idea. Twiss in particular hated wogs and he still regarded Johnny Mayhoe as an exception to prove the rule. Adams was always surprised at how fast Mayhoe got to the middle of a problem and how quickly he reacted when the problem was clear to him. He was the same on the street patrols or in the field. Adams wondered why the hell he'd joined the army.

'You're off your bleeding head,' said Twiss and locked his suitcase.

'Shurrup, Twissy,' said Mayhoe. 'Hang on a minute.' He picked up the photograph on Adams's locker. 'You got that to go back to, man. What's making you so fuckin' long in the face? She's a cracker, right?' Adams took the photo.

'Good bit of rumpo, Johnny. All wogs are, aren't they?' said Twiss and for a moment Mayhoe let the smile die out of his eyes. Twiss didn't notice and if he had he wouldn't have given a monkey's.

'I'm just wondering what it'll be like, that's all,' Adams said.

'What?' asked Mayhoe. 'What'll what be like, for Chrissakes?'

Adams put the photo back on the locker. 'Going home. You write letters, talk on the phone . . . She's been worried sick since I went.'

She'd begged to come with them and he'd refused. He'd made the excuse that they wouldn't get a billet together, that all the married quarters were gone. He didn't want her in Ireland and he'd made sure she didn't go.

'She could've come with us,' said Twiss. 'The other wives did.' Adams was surprised at the tone of accusation in Twiss's voice.

'Not your fuckin' business. I didn't want her there, that's all about it,' said Adams, and for a moment neither man said anything. Mayhoe broke the tension.

'You haven't seen her for six months, right?' Adams nodded. 'She's your bird, man. It'll be OK. My bird waits and she's not living with my mum and dad.' Mayhoe grinned.

Adams shook his head. 'That's it, Johnny,' he said. 'I'm not sure, not about her, but about going home. I don't want to go.'

He got up from the bed, picked up his crash hat and his kitbag and stood for a moment looking at the other two.

'Conquering hero, back from Ireland. They'll all be chuffed to fuck to see you, mate. Believe it,' said Mayhoe.

Adams nodded and walked quickly out of the barrack room.

'Wives,' said Twiss. 'Fucking hell.' He kicked the

65

door of his locker shut. 'You fit then, mate? Let's get that train. Eh?'

They stepped out onto the balcony that ran along the inner side of their block and watched Adams walking slowly across to the motorcycle park.

'You know what's getting up his nose?' said Twiss. Mayhoe watched Adams as he reached his bike and strapped on the kitbag.

'Nope,' he said. 'What is it?'

'That fucking kid, what's his name . . . the one that got it . . . the kid, just out of depot.' Twiss had already forgotten the man's name. It seemed to have happened months and months ago and yet it was only six days since the funeral. Tompkins hadn't any parents. He'd come into the army through a boys' home and had no one to send the bits to. Twiss had already put him completely out of his mind.

The engineers had arrived at the scene of the blast by the time Major Taylor and Sergeant-Major Gilby arrived. The Pig was completely gutted and was blocking the bridge. No one was going very close to it.

'What's on, Sergeant?' Major Taylor asked the engineer sergeant who was supervising the selection of the right towing gear.

'Nothing, sir. Not till Felix arrives, sir,' said the sergeant and Major Taylor nodded.

Felix would check that the whole area was clear before anyone tried towing the Pig clear. The ordnance team arrived within five minutes and began a detailed search for any other bombs. It was going to be a long night.

Major Taylor turned to Gilby and smiled a tight smile. 'Out man, would you say, Sergeant-Major?'

'Not sure, sir. Not his mark. Not big enough, is it?'

'We'll go back, I think.' The two men walked across

to their car and drove away.

'Don't understand it, sir,' said Gilby. 'Frank doesn't bother with poxy little things like that. I mean he was in luck with the Pig, maybe. But it's not his style.'

Major Taylor said nothing as they drove on towards their location.

'Maybe,' he eventually said dryly, 'maybe he's changed his style. Maybe he's running low on supplies. Maybe he thinks direct attacks on us is the answer.'

'And maybe it's not him at all, sir,' said Gilby. The two men watched the road. Gilby had the Browning on his lap and ready. Often incidents happened in pairs and he wasn't taking any chances. He'd shoot first and ask questions after, Gilby thought angrily.

They drove down the empty streets to Strathfelt, turned left across the bridge and the huge corrugated iron doors swung open. They drove through into the yard where Sergeant Bilinski was making sure that Gadd was handled gently as they took him out of the Pig. He'd had a bad and bumpy journey and those who'd been cramped into the back of the Pig had had their hands full trying to hold him still. He'd been lucky when he passed out.

Gilby walked quickly across to the sergeant. 'Well?' he said. 'All right?'

Bilinski just looked at him for a moment and then turned to Twiss and Mayhoe. 'Get yourselves inside. Debriefing in ten minutes?' He looked to Gilby for confirmation. The sergeant-major nodded.

'And Twiss, get us a cup of tea, will you?' Twiss nodded and followed Mayhoe into the building, trailing his rifle. He didn't even look at Sergeant-Major Gilby.

'A bastard,' said Gilby. Bilinski nodded. He was very tired now. He knew how lucky they were not to have lost anyone. It'd been close all right.

'That mad bomber, then, Sir?' he asked and Gilby

shook his head. 'I dunno,' said Gilby. 'Company commander seems to think it might be. I'm not sure.'

'Got to be,' said Bilinski. 'We've no one else in the area, have we? It's clean. You know that.'

Gilby shook his head. He had been looking forward to a quiet night. He'd almost begun to believe that Twiss had been wrong and that Frank wasn't in their patch. He'd been hoping against hope that nothing would happen until after they were all away and out of it. Now a bomb had gone off, a maker was around, someone who knew his job. It'd been deliberate, it'd been calculated and it'd worked. It wasn't the usual Irish cock-up, this one. If it was Frank they had trouble on their hands and if it wasn't it was worse in some ways because that meant they had a new boy on the loose and Intelligence wouldn't like that. They hated loose ends almost as much as Gilby did.

'I'll just sort out Gadd,' said Bilinski and Gilby stood aside to let the sergeant into the location. Twiss came out with two mugs of tea.

'You seen Sergeant Bilinski, sir?' he asked and Gilby nodded in the direction of the location. Twiss turned to follow his sergeant inside as Gilby took one of the mugs.

'I'll have the other one, soldier,' he said and took it. Twiss began to protest.

'Sir, that's my . . .' He let the sergeant-major have it. 'Major Taylor could use one, Twiss. OK?' he said and allowed his mouth to smile. Twiss walked quickly away into the dark doorway.

In the television room some of Recce Platoon were getting their heads down. 'Sod it,' said Adams as he leaned forward to undo his boots. 'A week on that fucking observation, we come off it one fucking hour and we get a fucking bomb.' He was angry. Jacko looked across at him and smiled.

'You win some, Adams,' he said, 'and you lose some.' He wiped his dirty hands across his eyes. They felt like

68

piss holes in the snow and he knew that all he wanted was a bath and bed and sleep for about forty-eight hours. Jacko also knew that he hadn't a hope in hell of getting it.

Other soldiers from B company were wandering about the room or playing cards and more were lying dozing in the battered armchairs grouped around the television. Adams wandered across to the tea urn and got a mug for himself.

'Colour?' he asked and Jackson nodded. They drank their tea without speaking again. Adams felt his head dropping forward onto the table and he jerked himself awake as Tom Gilby walked across to them.

'You hear about it, then?' asked the sergeant-major and Jacko nodded.

'Bastard,' said Gilby. 'Gadd's got a busted leg. Not good.'

'We heard,' said Jackson.

'Is Captain Simmons around?' Gilby asked.

'No, he's with Mr Preece. They're trying to sort out some other OPs. Recce platoon is a bit pushed. Sorry about it, but there you are.'

Gilby shrugged. 'You know that woman came through the vehicle check point just before they moved off?'

'Yes.' Jackson sighed. 'Was she clean?'

'As a whistle. Nothing in the car. Bilinski gave it a good going over. Nothing in the car.'

'She might've detonated the bomb. If it was waiting for her. Right?'

The sergeant-major nodded. 'Frank makes it, someone delivers it and someone else presses the tit. Neat, and little chance of anyone getting picked up. It's neat all right.'

'Our man?' asked Jackson.

'I don't give a monkey's who it was,' said Gilby angrily. 'I just want the bastard nailed up.'

'I thought you wanted a quiet last few days, sir,' said Jacko.

69

'I did. We've a man wounded, Jacko. Not his fault, he might've been dead. Next time someone could be. I want him, whoever it is, and he's lucky I can't get a few minutes with him before he gets handed over.'

'Rules and regulations, Tom,' said Jackson smiling. 'Fuck them,' said the sergeant-major and then he shook his head. 'Right. Rules and regulations.' He smiled at Jacko. 'And you lot withdraw your observation post. Bloody hell,' he said.

'It was agreed. Major Taylor, Lieutenant Preece . . . it was agreed, Tom.'

'A mistake, wasn't it?'

Adams watched the two men. He knew they were friends and he'd never seen the sergeant-major so cold, so angry. Adams knew Gilby was efficient, knew he was a good soldier and he didn't trust him because he was cold as ice. Nothing ever seemed to make him laugh. Not openly.

'We were going back tomorrow morning for a twelve-hour and if nothing happened after that . . . lift it completely,' said Jackson.

'Bolting the stable door, Jacko,' said Gilby. Jackson drank the last of the tea.

'I thought Frank went in for the big stuff. Lorries full of it,' said Jackson.

Gilby nodded. 'Maybe he's trying a new technique. I dunno. But there is someone and that's all we need to know. Except where the fucking hell to find him in this Irish bog.'

Adams got up and walked out of the room. He'd had enough of the whole business. He walked into the mess room, cooked himself a steak and joined Mayhoe, Twiss, Box and Hunt at their table.

On the other side of the room he noticed the new kid, Tompkins, who was watching the group around the centre table. They were all laughing as Twiss went on with a story.

'Went over with one hell of a fucking bang, man. Me and Mayhoe get back across the bridge fast when they tell us no one's seen Gaddy. He's got to be inside, right? He was too. Fast akip. Mayhoe kissed him and he woke up and bust his leg from shock. Fancy being kissed by Jomo here, eh? eh?' He laughed again and the others joined him. Adams sat down. He was almost too tired to laugh. Twiss suddenly noticed that Tompkins was looking at them.

'What're you staring at, sonny?' Twiss asked and he wasn't laughing any more. Tompkins shook his head.

'Me?' he said. 'Nothing.'

'You were. You were looking at me. Weren't you? You looking for something, are you?' Twiss stood up and stared at the youngster.

'Knock it off, man,' said Mayhoe and put a hand on Twiss's arm. Twiss shook it off.

I don't like being fucking stared at, Jomo. Right? Look funny, do I, sonny? You go without kip as long as I have, you get to look funny.'

'I wasn't looking at you, straight up,' said the youngster. He was afraid of Twiss and didn't know how to get out of the situation. He'd heard that Twiss was a punchy bastard and that he'd be happy to have any excuse to put the boot in. Twiss grinned. He was enjoying himself. Tompkins was a good target.

'Been here long, have you?' Tompkins shook his head. 'So fuckin' don't stare at us. All right?' Twiss sat down still looking at Tompkins, who slowly looked away. 'Know what I like best?' Twiss went on to the group around the table.

'The sound of your own voice,' said Adams and grinned.

'Own goals,' said Twiss. 'When it's the bloody makers who get it from their own fucking bombs. I like that. Raises a cheer that does. An own goal. I hate bombers

71

like I hate fucking starers.' He stared again across at the young soldier. 'You wait till you've done an eighteen-month and a couple of four-months out here, sonny.'

Adams looked across at the boy. The lad was scared. 'Take no notice, he's a bit shook up, that's all.'

'Who is?' asked Twiss angrily.

'Oh shurrup, knock it off,' said Adams and cut into his steak. For a moment no one spoke. Their young faces were grey, their eyes dead from lack of sleep, their minds stopped by the sheer inertia they all felt. They wanted out now OK. Days-to-do happy they might be and they'd count those days off the calendar one by one. Twiss began to laugh.

'What's up now?' Mayhoe asked.

'You see Caddy's face when we pulled him out, Jomo?

Bloody hell, I thought we'd torn his leg off.' Mayhoe began to smile and then to laugh too. Adams got up and walked across to Tompkins and sat down. 'Who are you, anyway?' , he asked.

'Just got sent.'

'Hard luck,' said Adams. 'What do they call you?'

'They said it'd be good experience. Back in depot. Said it'd be good to get a taste. Tompkins.'

Adams nodded and sniffed. This kid, what, eighteen? sent out for experience. Not fair on him. Not fair on his mates either. No experience on the streets and you could be a liability. He was scared too, this one. Still they all were, first time out.

'D'you hear that?' Adams called across to the others. 'Sent him for experience. Bastard base rats.'

'Experience,' snorted Twiss. 'Stuff it. We just lost a Pig, that's experience. A laugh an' all. If you get out.' Twiss turned to the rest. 'Tea? All round?' He looked across at Tompkins. 'You?' he asked.

The boy nodded, pleased to be asked. 'You get them

in, sonny Jim,' said Twiss grinning. 'Wet behind the fucking ears.' The boy walked away to the urn to get their tea. They were all laughing at him.

'And you're not, I suppose, Twiss?' Sergeant-Major Gilby was standing at the door. 'Or you, Adams? Eh?'

'I'm wet all bloody right, sir,' said Adams. 'Soaked. Lying on that bloody hillside for nothing.'

'Complaining, Adams?' Sergeant-Major Gilby walked into the room. He didn't like Adams. Didn't like his manner, didn't rate him and reckoned he wasn't worth a light. It didn't do to show it and he tried not to, but Gilby knew that Adams resented him too.

'I was taking bets, sir. That's all.'

'What bets?' Gilby asked.

'That we were enjoying it more being pissed on in that Irish bog than you lot were down here in the town. That's all, sir.'

Gilby stared at Adams for a moment then, 'You two,' he said and turned to Mayhoe and Twiss.

'I didn't do it, sir,' said Mayhoe automatically. 'Nothing to do with us!'

'Not the way Sergeant Bilinski tells it. You did well. Quick, got him out, no messing, in and out like we like it. Next time, think. That's all. Wait for the order and watch for secondaries. That's all.'

He'd been pleased to have his opinion of Twiss confirmed. Twiss was trouble, sure. Twiss could be a bully, for certain, but Sergeant-Major Gilby saw in the hardness of the young soldier a quality that he knew to be in himself. Twiss was a ruthless bastard. Both soldiers seemed to be pleased that for once he wasn't reaming them out. 'Very good,' he said. Tompkins came back with a tray, slopping tea all over it. He put the tray down on the table and they each took one. Sergeant-Major Gilby took one too, leaving Tompkins with nothing. His face fell and those sitting around the table, those who'd been here so long and so many times, laughed at him. He was a wet-eared, red-arse and not worth a gob in the wind was Tompkins.

'Get some fucking time in,' said Twiss and they all laughed again.

It was later that evening. Down the hill and across the road a single light burned in the window of the farmhouse. The woman was going to her bed. She stood for a moment at the window and stared out at the dark, poor land. Nothing moved across the dark night. No noise broke the silence and the moon was hidden now behind black clouds that moved hugely across the sky. She turned from the window and got into the cold bed. For a moment before she put the light out she thought about Frank and about the van under the bridge, then she turned on her side, reached out for the switch and the room was dark too. Soon it began to rain.

Jacko and Tom Gilby sat in the back of the Land Rover together and talked above the roar of the engine. They'd a man riding shot-gun and Gilby now had his rifle. Jacko fiddled with the SLR between his knees. Major Taylor had suggested he should take the chance of a cabby up to Stranmoore. 'Get off, Colour Sergeant. Go and see your wife. You'll not be wanted on the OP till the morning.' Jacko was tired and pleased to get back to Mary and the kids even for a short time. Mary'd be pleased to see him, thought Jacko. He hadn't been back in camp more than five nights in the last month. She didn't complain but he knew that she felt the strain as much as they all did.

'You'll be glad to be off tonight, Jacko. Pissing down. Look at it.' They drove on past the farm which lay in darkness and on up the mountain road to the camp. It was a dangerous route to take and a number of illegal road blocks had been set up along the mountain stretch. Major Taylor had insisted on the extra man to ride escort. He was taking no chances of another ambush on his company.

74

'How does Mary take it, Jacko?' Gilby asked.

Jackson shrugged. 'No complaints, Tom,' he said.

'No place for a woman, this,' said Gilby. Jacko grinned at him.

'They choose to come, Tom. Up to them.'

'Bullshit. One comes, they all come. Bloody sheep.'

'Women?' asked Jacko innocently. He loved to get Tom Gilby going on the subject. He was curiously shy of women and it was only recently that he'd seemed to be at ease with Mary. Maybe he could feel her reserve about him. Jacko didn't know.

'Fact, Jacko,' said the sergeant-major and he stared bleakly out of the back of the Land Rover.

'Don't go,' he went on. 'Not with the job.'

'I dunno. I'm all right.'

'Sure you are. You feel lucky, that's all. She'll do you no harm.'

Jacko laughed. 'I'll tell her you said so.'

Gilby looked across at him seriously. 'I meant it,' he said flatly.

For a moment the Land Rover slowed and both men were instantly alert. The driver looked round at them. 'Nothing, sir. Just a dog, I think.' Gilby sniffed and shifted the rifle to ease the weight. He was pissed off tonight. Major Taylor had really got his teeth into this bomber business. 'He wants him, Jacko. Us due out soon and he wants the bastard nailed up.'

'A blaze of glory?' Jacko asked. Gilby shrugged.

'A job done. Rounded off, that's what he said.'

Jacko shook his head. Neither man said anything for a time. Gilby patted his pockets looking for a cigarette, didn't find one and remembered that Jacko didn't smoke. He'd have to go without.

Jacko was angry about the bomb. He was sure the woman was involved. She'd gone through the check point at the right time. Maybe she was clean but he wished they could put the screws on her.

'Getting impatient, Tom. Must be old age. In a hurry. Or just plain soft.' Gilby didn't say anything and for a time they drove on in silence. Outside the slash of the wheels through water reminded them that it was still sheeting down. He was glad to be going home to a warm bed. He wondered what Gilby had to look forward to. A drink maybe, but he drank little; a chat in the Sergeants' Mess, except that there'd be few people in just now. It seemed to Jacko that Tom Gilby had a bleak bed to lie in. Nothing but the army the whole of his life. Thin feast indeed.

'We don't have enough blokes to go round, Jacko. And even if we do find him for Major Taylor what'll we bloody do with him? Pat him on the head and threaten him with court. They go away laughing.'

'What would you do, Tom?' Jacko asked. The sergeant-major looked at him casually. 'The same as you, Jacko. The same as you.'

'No, you wouldn't, Tom. We'd both like to thump the five colours of shit out of him but we won't, will we?' The sergeant-major sniffed and shook his head a fraction.

'Not politics, Jacko. No. And don't let Major Taylor hear you say what you'd like to do either. Or you'll have blighted your chances. Right?'

Jackson looked across at Gilby in surprise. 'What's that supposed to mean then, Tom?' he asked.

'Men in command, Jacko,' said the sergeant-major, 'have to stay schtum, understand the situation and stop their men feeling too aggressive. A low-key operation. Something like that.'

'I can have an opinion, can't I?' The two men were having to shout against the roar of the engine as the Land Rover laboured up the steepest part of the mountain road. The wind blew steadily across the road and any trees that grew here were gnarled and bent. The headlights of the Land Rover picked out outcrops of rock that showed

76

through the thin soil. Water ran spurting down the mountain and across the road, making the going treacherous.

Gilby stared speculatively at the rifle in his hand. He had wind of changes to come and he didn't like them. But then Jacko was a friend and he might as well be told now by Gilby. He might remember the favour sometime and that could do no harm. Jacko was a high flyer and Gilby wasn't ashamed of hitching his wagon to a thruster.

'Can't I?' repeated Jacko. Gilby looked up at him and sighed.

'Perhaps. But not if there's promotion in the wind. Not if you want it, that is.' Jackson waited for him to go on. 'Not exactly promotion, in fact. Platoon commander's job.; When we get back to Tidworth a platoon in each company is ; to have an NCO commander. Could be you for one of them, Jacko.' He smiled at Jackson. 'Silk purses out of sows' ears.'

'Nice,' said Jackson. 'Your opinion?'

Gilby smiled. I'm not paid to have an opinion, am I, Jacko?' he said. 'Mary'd be chuffed as little apples, wouldn't! she?' he went on. Jacko shifted in his seat.

'*I'd* be chuffed as little apples. A platoon.' He could feel the excitement he'd last felt when he was made up to lance-jack so long back. Real step up the ladder, this. She'd be pleased all right. 'How the hell d'you know, Tom?' he asked. 'You're not kidding around, are you?'

'Me?' Gilby asked innocently. 'Would I? Just heard that's all, Jacko. Thought you'd be pleased. How d'you get on with Sergeant Bilinski?'

'All right. You know him better than me. He's in your company, isn't he?' Gilby nodded.

'It's just a whisper, Jacko. No more. Many a slip and all that.' Gilby sat back against the side of the Land Rover and watched Jacko chewing it over. He was pleased and so he should be. He was getting the nod from the CO and the other senior ranks that they had an eye on him. Gilby thought bitterly of his own situation. No one had pushed him. He'd got where he was by hard work, steel and determination. It hadn't been that easy. He'd had no easy commands, no real encouragement. He was suddenly aware of how bitter he felt about the job. They'd toss him out when they thought he was no use. It wasn't the army; it was just that they didn't care for him. Gilby wasn't being sentimental or self-pitying but objective about himself. It wasn't easy to face the sort of facts he was facing. Jacko would go far, maybe take a commission. That's what his wife would want. Gilby smiled at the pressure Jacko would be under from that wife. Ambitious, scheming and determined to make the Officers' Mess, the sherry-party circuit, Gilby thought bitterly. He wondered which way Jacko would want to jump. If he took a commission, right now, he might make major. No further, not now. It'd take a real war for him to make anything more than major. Maybe he'll do it. Depends on that woman. Gilby glanced across at Jacko and was amused by the look of intense thought that was covering the colour-sergeant's face. Jacko looked across at him.

'What do you think, Tom?'

Gilby shrugged. I'm not paid to think too much, Jacko. I told you before. I do a job.'

The Land Rover arrived at the perimeter wire of the Stranmoore camp. The arc lights burned through the night to deter any of the bastards who might want to chuck a bomb into the married quarters, or who might try for a raid on the armoury. Not that they needed to. Not with the money they got from their collections. If it isn't guns bought by US money, it's guns bought by the profiteers and money men on both sides, Gilby thought angrily. Getting arms is never a problem.

They drove past the guardroom and stopped at the unloading bay. They got out of the back of the Land Rover to check their weapons. Jacko was getting a lift to his quarter.

'Oh, Jacko.' Gilby leaned in at the back of the vehicle. 'Don't count your chickens, will you? We've still got some time yet.'

He stepped away in the pool of light outside the armoury door. The rain streaked down past the lights in almost solid sheets. Jacko shivered.

'OK, drive on. The sergeant-major's walking,' he said.

They drove slowly across the old runway and around the main complex, past the gym in the converted hangar and past the Officers' Mess. A few lights still burned in the bar but there would be almost no one there except base rats. The Sergeants' Mess stood at the end of the first row of married quarters. They drove faster now and Jacko was glad. He wanted to see Mary. They'd need to talk that bit of information over.

In the farmhouse that same evening the woman wasn't sleeping well. She knew that she had set the alarm but she never slept well when she had a job to do. It'd been quiet for months until Frank came back. Now she hardly saw him and he never came near the house. She wasn't happy about it, but there wasn't much she could do. It was something she had to put up with. Anyway he was busy and she was glad of the work she could do to help. He was a quiet man and gentle, and when he'd lived with her she'd been happier than she had thought possible. They thought the same, believed in the same things, and she'd never accepted it when people said he was just using her. He had a cause and she was happy to fight with him.

The clock ticked away quietly on the bedside table. She reached out into the cold room for it, looked at the luminous fingers. Twelve. Another five hours to wait before she had to go. She turned over, clutching the clock, and fell asleep.

Jacko walked quietly into the living-room of their married quarters. Mary was sitting in the armchair, asleep. The television hummed in the corner and it was obvious she'd been put to sleep by it. He quietly walked over, turned it off and went through into the kitchen. It was the thud of the fridge door that woke her. He walked back into the room with a can of beer in his hand. He was grinning like a cat with the cream. 'I haven't sat down all day,' he said, quoting her. 'On my feet . . .'

She didn't move, just sat and stared at him. 'Pig,' she said and then got out of the chair and over to him. 'What are you doing here?'

'Looking for your fancy man. What else?' he said and kissed her. She wouldn't let him go. She clung to him hard and when he finally stepped away from her she still held his arm.

'Hey, love, what's up?' he asked. She smiled and shook her head. 'It's all right.'

'A couple of hours, love,' he said. 'Tom brought me back. Time for a shower, something to eat. Just.'

She reached up and kissed him again. He didn't respond. 'You're tired,' she said.

'Yes,' he said. 'Very.'

She shook her head. 'It's always the same, Jacko. You come back screwed up. Every time it's the same. I'm not complaining, love, I just . . . It's not very easy, is it?'

It was the same for all of them. They talked about it whenever they met for those awful coffee mornings. All the wives found it. Their men came back edgy, irritable, still wearing the defensive attitudes they'd developed for their work. The wives hated what it did to their marriages.

'I'm glad you're back, Jack. That's all.' He nodded and moved away to the door. 'I'll have a word with the kids.'

'You will not. You wake them and you can put them

80

back to bed. They'll never go to sleep. Look at them all right but don't you dare wake them.'

Jackson smiled. 'OK. Bring us another beer up, will you?'

The rain began to ease off. Jacko lay in bed staring at the ceiling and listened to it. He'd have to get up soon and get back to the location. Tom Gilby had promised to call by for him on his way back to base camp in Strathfelt.

Beside him Mary lay on her side. He looked across at her. It'd been no good again. Every time he came back they tried to make love and every time he messed it up. She was very patient and kind about it but Jacko knew she was upset. Everything was too hurried. A moment snatched and always ticking away in the back of his head the knowledge that he'd soon be back on an OP or doing a search or making a detailed report at a debriefing session. The war in Ireland percolated through to every aspect of their lives, so that even the simple act of love was screwed up by it. Jacko's mouth tightened in anger. He hadn't told Mary the news that Gilby had given him. If anything happened to put the blocks on she'd only be disappointed. He'd decided to keep the news to himself until it was confirmed.

Mary lay still. She was wide awake and knew that Jacko was too. She was sorry about the loving. She'd always enjoyed him and now they had to suffer again this biting anguish of not being able to make it together. They didn't talk about this at the coffee mornings or in the NAAFI shop when the wives met. They didn't talk about it when the padre made a routine call or when the CO's wife came and chatted. They didn't even talk to their husbands about it. Mary didn't believe that she and Jack were the only people with the problem but she still felt isolated and lonely. She tried, she tried very hard to make him relax, to help him, but the fact was that nothing she did helped. Whatever was stopping him, whatever was screwing him

81

up was in his head and she couldn't get through to him. Ireland and the war were too much of a strain for any marriage to bear, and yet they went on with it.

Mary often wondered, when she was alone, if her mother and father had been right. 'He's not, well, your type, darling,' her mother had said and she had really meant, he's not your class. 'My dear girl, a corporal in the infantry . . . I mean, how will you talk to him? Marriage isn't just attraction, you know, it's more than that.' Mary stared at the wall blindly now and wondered if they had been right. She'd been with Jacko a dozen years and he'd done well. Her father had come to like him in a reserved way and her mother had stopped making the snobbish comments which had usually been reserved for their visits home. But lying in bed in this quarter beside the man she suddenly felt that she didn't know anything about him. He had a part of his life so separate, so dislocated from hers. She felt bitterly that no one who wasn't an army wife could even begin to understand.

The fighting in Ireland involved the wives, sucked them along as a matter of loyalty. They had the choice of coming or not, and almost all the wives had come. It was perhaps a gesture, by some, of their love for their husbands; others came because they felt a certain loyalty to the regiment too. It had made one difference, this fighting. The regiment was a unit again and the army wives were part of that, whether they liked it or not.

Mary shut her eyes. She didn't want to be just an 'army wife'. She wanted an identity that was her own. She didn't want to be merely the partner of a soldier. Jack was a fine man. He was strong, protective, gave her as much rope as she wanted, paid the bills, was good with the kids . . . or he had been. In the past eighteen months he had changed. He was colder, more calculating, shorter-tempered and often seething with a rage that he couldn't discuss with her. He'd sit, on his occasional nights at home, staring at the television or a newspaper and he wouldn't be seeing them. Mary resented that. She was cut off from the experience he was going through and she felt cheated by circumstances. She hated Ireland now because it was through the fighting here that the strains and pressures on their marriage had become physical. She ached to be had by him and she knew that it was useless to try. She turned over towards him.

'It'll be better in England, Jacko. Better for us. Won't it?'

He didn't say anything for a moment and even when he spoke he didn't look at her. I'm sorry,' he said.

She touched him gently. 'Come on, love. You're still on that OP, aren't you? It doesn't help.'

Jacko sighed and stirred a little. He looked across at her and grinned suddenly. 'Eyes like a panda's. Binoculars to your skull eight hours. It's crackers. We are,' he said and took her hands. She was warm beside him and he knew that she wanted loving as much as he wanted it, but something wouldn't break inside him. Something held him back.

'None of us enjoy it, Jack. It's not long, though, now. Not long.'

'I spend days on that hillside . . . just thinking. You know.' She lay in the warm dark of the bed and said nothing. He hadn't talked about the work before. He'd wanted to keep it away from her and she had never asked.

'All sorts of things. The work, you, the kids . . . all sort of jumbled up.' Jacko found it hard to put into words. He wasn't used to talking about his thoughts to anyone, not even to Mary. He suddenly realized that he had never really talked about the job to her. Nor to anyone. Not what he felt about it, not what he thought would happen, not about any of it.

'Just sitting there waiting for some stupid woman to do something. Lead us somewhere. And all the time you're

83

back here. It's stupid.'

'You enjoy it, Jacko. Don't pretend.'

'I'm not pretending,' he said angrily. 'I . . . I was talking to Adams. He's not a bad soldier. He was thinking the same. That's all.'

'Why didn't he bring his wife?'

'Dunno. That's up to him. He didn't want her to come.' He knew how Mary would feel. She hadn't been happy to bring the kids this time. She'd only come, he knew, because she felt he wanted her to, expected the loyalty from her that he valued so highly.

'Nothing to do with us, that. She didn't come, that's all, but he's sitting in the rain and laughing and thinking the same as me. I just don't know why the hell we stand it.'

Mary put a hand to his mouth. She knew that Jacko needed to get away, that eighteen months of strain in the locations and in the streets and countryside were demanding too much from any man. It was almost as if it'd be easier if the women had not come. They added to the pressures the men were under.

'It's all right, Jacko. Don't talk about it now.'

'I think that woman I'm watching, she's bait. Oh, yeah. That's all she is. I'm thinking, she's a bitch. She helps a bloke, someone we're looking for. We know that. Do we know why? Or what she feels for him? No. Not our job to know. She must be mad because she is helping a man. We make the, I dunno, the equation. Somehow.'

He lay back in the dark and rubbed his hands over his eyes. He felt drained by it all. He knew he would be glad to get away this time. More glad than he had ever been to get out of anywhere. There were some soldiers who volunteered to come back on tour after tour. Some who reckoned it was what soldiering was about. Jacko didn't.

'You've all simple minds, Jacko,' Mary said quietly. He turned towards her.

84

'I don't believe that. You don't believe that. Do you?'

Mary hesitated a moment and then sighed. 'Black is black, white is white . . .'

For a moment he was silent. They'd never talked about it before and he wasn't sure he wanted to now. He was very much afraid that Mary would begin to question the basis on which he worked.

'You don't really think that we think like that?'

Mary took his hand and kissed the hard knuckles. He shut his eyes for a moment and waited.

'I wouldn't be here if I did. You just have to let it go sometimes, love. That's all. Forget it. Don't let it sit on your back.' Mary was afraid. She knew that whatever she said now had to be chosen carefully, for she could destroy the shell he had built around himself and his work. Mary knew by instinct how dangerous this would be. 'I can't do your job. I wouldn't want to. I can't even share it. Different worlds, different views, different everything, really. You see, love?' she said.

Apart from the rain, which had almost stopped, the night was silent. A guard dog howled in the compound by the Sergeants' Mess. Then there was silence in the whole camp. The only lights apart from those around the fences were the ones burning in the guardroom. Beyond the camp, in the country, Jacko knew that another OP had been set up and that tomorrow he would be back observing that farm and the woman whose face he knew from an identity photograph taken months before. For a moment he wondered what she was like, but he crushed the thought almost as soon as it came. It didn't matter what she was like. All that mattered was that she helped a dangerous man, a killer. The only woman he had ever really known lay quietly beside him, holding his hand to her breast. He looked across at her and he felt desperation deep in him.

'So,' he asked. 'Why are you here?'

She turned quietly to him, put her arms round him and

pulled his head down to her. He reached blindly for her warm body as she kissed him. 'Why?' he asked again.

'Just because,' she whispered gently and they lay quietly together and forgot Ireland, and the men on the OP, and loyalty, and for a moment thought only about themselves.

The alarm rang in the woman's hand and she woke quickly, killed the shrilling noise and pushed the warm blankets away. In the cold house she dressed, quietly picked up her car keys from the dressing-table and walked downstairs. She had no time for a cup of tea if she was going to do her work. She had no doubt that she would find the car where she had been told. She had no doubt that Frank would have done his part. She didn't understand why he was undertaking such small and apparently useless operations. She didn't ask when they met. Frank knew what he was doing and that was enough.

She'd loved him, still did, but he'd gone cold on her as he became more and more involved with the struggle. He believed in the fight more than he believed in anything else, and his determination stamped out any need for love or gentleness in his life. She regretted so much, and yet she felt that the only thing she could now offer him was her loyalty. She did as she was asked and she felt that this, perhaps, could bring her close to him again. Perhaps he was using her but this way they met, they talked together, and even if he no longer lay in her bed it almost didn't matter. Outside it was cold and she shivered in the sudden rush of damp wind as she opened the back door of the house. Nothing moved in the yard, nothing broke the silence of the hills and the dark forest beyond the road. She felt alone and yet curiously safe. Nothing would go wrong, no one could know that he was back, no one could make a connection, therefore, between the two of them. It was, in its way, exhilarating. She drove her car slowly up the

86

track.

Nothing stirred on the edge of the trees. There was no one there now and nothing left to show they had been except the flattened indentations in the pine needles at the edge of the tree line and a couple of wrappers from sticks of gum. She drove carefully out onto the main road and turned towards her target.

Chapter Five

That same morning Twiss and Mayhoe sat at the back of the room with the rest of Six Platoon and waited for Major Taylor to give them a briefing. They were all very angry. One of their mates had been hit and it wasn't going to be easy to cool their tempers. They'd had enough of playing patsy with the situation and they wanted some action.

Sergeant Bilinski looked around the crowded room and watched the tense, pale faces of the soldiers as they waited in silence for the briefing session to begin. He knew that Major Taylor had chosen to give the briefing this morning because he was aware of how bitter the men felt. The platoon needed calming down and Major Taylor was going to have his hands full trying to do it.

The room was already stuffy when Captain Simmons gave them permission to smoke. Bilinski glanced across at the young officer and grinned. He'd gauged the mood too, and knew that he had to relax the atmosphere.

Tompkins sat near Corporal Box and played nervously with a lighter. He glanced about the room at the other men and couldn't read the fear he felt in their faces. The captain, perched on the edge of the table, looked tired out, as they all did. Somehow sleep didn't help any more. Captain Simmons yawned widely and smiled across at Bilinski, who was watching him. 'Need some more bed, Sergeant,' he said. He'd been working in the locations night after night and the sergeant knew he'd spent more nights planning patrols than in his bed in barracks. He didn't seem scared of anything and certainly pushed himself as hard as he pushed the men of B company.

The recce section sat apart from the others. They knew better than anyone the toughness of their next assignment.

Just to locate the bomber was going to be hard enough, but to get even enough evidence to make any charges stick would be even harder. Colour-Sergeant Jackson sat sprawled in his chair behind one of the plastic-topped tables and chatted quietly to Adams. Bilinski knew that recce section regarded itself as something special, and in a way it was. They were specially chosen from the battalion and they did a job that .required very particular skills.

It wasn't a simple 'us and them' situation like Aden or Malaya. It was a bloody miracle, Bilinski reckoned, that there hadn't been more incidents like Bloody Sunday. It was a bloody miracle that they'd managed, in the time their battalion had been in the area, to make some contact with the locals of both sides. Bilinski knew that the contact was always tinged with suspicion of the motives of the army. It wasn't his business to ask why or when or how. As far as Sergeant Bilinski was concerned, things were clear. They were here to help the police and to keep the community from each other's throats. It was a bastard of a job without getting bothered about who was right or who was wrong. But he knew that the contacts they had made were fragile and that unless Six Platoon were given it straight by Major Taylor this morning they'd stand a chance of losing those contacts. It took only one kid to throw a stone, or one yobbo to shout at them, or a bunch of women to stand and spit at them and they might go bang. He knew there'd be little but his discipline holding them if they did get mad and had an excuse to let loose. It'd be ugly and it'd screw up the work of nearly eighteen months.

There were some who reckoned the only thing was to get stuck in and screw the consequences. It hadn't been their policy and Bilinski wished they'd fly Six Platoon out, man and gun, today, before they put them back on the job.

The men stood up as Major Taylor walked in.

'Sit,' he said and turned to face them after nodding at Captain Simmons and Bilinski.

The men sat down and waited for him to speak. Major Taylor spoke quietly and without any emotion. He too was angry at the incident at the bridge and he was determined to get the people responsible before the company left the Province. But he knew that Six Platoon were punchy, under great strain, and very angry.

'The first thing, Gadd is comfortable. He'll be playing football in a month. He'd better be.' He smiled at them and the men sat back a little and some of the tension went.

'You had a nasty go last night. I don't want it to affect you. This area is quiet and I want it to stay that way. Not least because we're going out in a week and I don't want another casualty in that time.' He looked around the room. They were listening to him and, he hoped, taking it in. It was a good platoon, this, if it had the right leadership. They were hard and they were experienced men, and he hoped they'd absorb what he was saying.

'People get slack in the last few days before leaving. Fact. They disregard the normal rules of security and when they do, they get hit. They're not fools we're dealing with and their Intelligence is good enough to know that we are due to finish next week. They'll be trying to trigger off some action before we go. I want our activity here to remain low-key. Understand?'

The men said nothing. They knew what he was telling them and they didn't like it. They were being asked to sit back and take the provocation and to do and say nothing. It wasn't what they wanted.

'You are all angry. I am angry. A mate got hurt and a vehicle damaged. All right, we're angry. But it won't do to lose our tempers. It'll do damn all good and I want you to remember that.' He paused and looked along the rows of faces. The men in the room said nothing. He knew that they were anxious to have a go at anything or anybody. It was the normal reaction of a soldier to want to respond to violence with violence. That was the name of the game for these lads. It was what they were trained to do. He went on very quietly. 'But one thing, I want that bomber. Understand? I want him.' He smiled thinly and stopped. At the back of the room Corporal Box stood up.

'Yes, Corporal?' said Major Taylor.

'Just one thing, sir,' said the Welshman. 'If we find him, what do we do?'

Major Taylor leaned forward across the table. 'Just find him, Corporal Box. Just find him.'

The corporal hesitated and then said, 'Do we bring him in, sir?' The rest of the men nodded, and began to murmur among themselves.

Major Taylor looked across at Captain Simmons who shook his head a fraction.

'You find him and under no circumstances let him know he's spotted. I don't want our bird to fly. When we nail him up it'll be for good and all and we want, the case to stick.'

The soldiers wanted more than this. They wanted revenge. They knew who the bomb maker was, they knew his carriers, or one of them, they knew all they felt necessary and yet they couldn't just get stuck into him and put him away. Major Taylor had a certain sympathy with their view.

'It will do the usual rounds, the RUC, court and, if we've got the evidence, prison. We'll get no evidence if we just snatch him off the street. He'll shut up and none of his contacts will blow the gaff. That's something we have to live with. A court would throw it out and he'd go free and laughing. We'll make sure it sticks. Right?'

A muted murmur of agreement came from the men. Twiss stared at the ceiling and didn't bother to listen to the rest. He wanted ten minutes with the bastard before they handed him over, that's all he wanted. Major Taylor left Captain Simmons to give them a more detailed briefing and Sergeant Bilinski to divide Six Platoon into a couple of patrols, one of which was to do routine street patrols and the other to go out into the country for their patrols. A third section would be on stand-by in the location in case anything came up.

In the meantime the woman had done her work well. She drove slowly back along the country road towards her farm. Her mother and father had tried to scratch a living from the land but it had been a hopeless business. Nothing good would grow in the thin, acid soil and there was no money for modernizing the equipment they used. Her father had been a bitter man as he grew older and her mother hardly spoke from one day's end to the next. By the time Frank appeared her father had been buried three years. The woman was bitter because she felt he would have enjoyed Frank and that he would have been pleased that she was joining in the struggle for something better than he had ever had. Her mother had hated Frank and when he moved into the house she never spoke again, either to her daughter or to the man. It'd been an ugly going her mother had had, and the woman shut her eyes a moment when she remembered the anger and the hatred that had lain buried for so long in her mother. She had been destroyed by her life on the land. She had worked unceasingly to get something out of the farm and she had failed. It had been a cold place and an ugly place to grow up in and the woman resented that. But more she resented the jealousy that her mother had felt for Frank. He was a good, kind man and he had come to her not only for a place to hide out but also for peace and gentleness. When the old woman died Frank had not been there for the British had him in prison and when he came out he hadn't bothered to make any contact for months and months. It was as if the death of the old woman had forced him away from her and she didn't understand that.

She'd found the car easily enough, parked outside a pub on the main road into town. It was an isolated place and it seemed stupid to her that Frank should want to waste a bomb on the place. But she did as she had been told, set the timer and walked quickly away to where she had parked. No one had seen her, it was much too early for anyone to be out and the dawn had been a cold and wet one. All she knew about the pub was that some informer had been known to use the place and that occasionally the army would put an Intelligence man in there to gather information. That was what she was told and she believed Frank when he told her anything. 'Just to warn the other bastards who might think of betraying us,' said Frank.

She didn't know who drove the car and the bomb into position and it wasn't her business to ask. Perhaps Frank did it but she doubted that. He'd a team of active men and women who did not know each other, so that there were natural cut offs all along the line. Frank liked organizing and he had made careful studies of resistance and guerrilla operations before he became active in the area. Now that he'd been put away once it was even more important that nothing could lead back to him.

She checked her watch. It'd go up in ten minutes and by that time she'd be back at the house.

That same morning found recce section back in its OP over looking the farm. They'd moved into position, camouflage themselves and their equipment, and moved quietly back into the spaces they had come to know too well.

Colour-Sergeant Jackson checked that his men were in position and took up the handset.

'Hello, two, this is six zero bravo. Over.'

He listened to the request for a situation report and wipe his hand across his blackened face. Jacko looked across at Adams who was scanning the farmhouse with the glasses.

'In position. Everything very quiet. Out.' He shut do

the set and crawled across to lie alongside Adams who was still checking the buildings across the road.

'Well?' asked Jackson. 'All still, is it?'

'Yeah,' said Adams. 'Too fucking still. I can't see her car.' He handed the glasses to the colour-sergeant and put his head down on his arms. The smell of the pine needles rose to meet him from the damp earth. He liked it up here away from the location. Down there he felt cramped, but here although he might be wet and cold at least he had some fresh air, and the sickness of the job they were doing in the town and the conditions under which they lived could be forgotten.

Colour spent a long time checking the buildings and could find no sign of the car. It could be at the back of the house and he was about to send Hunt off to check when a low whistle from his left alerted him. Hunt was pointing down the main road. The woman's car was driving slowly down the main road from the direction of the border.

'Shit,' said Jackson and Adams looked sharply at him. 'We should've stayed on all night, Colour,' he said.

Jackson sniffed, picked up the car in the glasses. It was the woman all right. The car turned off the road and along the track.

Jackson handed the glasses back to Private Adams as the woman got out of the car and walked into the house.

'Watch her,' he said and moved quickly away from the soldier and back to the handset. He wanted a quick word now with Recce Platoon commander. 'Hello, two, six zero bravo. Over.'

He waited for a response under the canopy of fir trees. They were black against the dull light of the early morning sun. They dripped suddenly onto the carpet of needles underfoot.

'Two nine, this is two. Over.' Colour-Sergeant Jackson cursed their luck. If they'd been on at night and seen her go out they'd've known where she went. If they'd

94

been on they could have put a tail on her, checked her movements. Now they weren't going to know if she'd told the truth to the VCP under Sergeant Bilinski the night before. Did she stay with her uncle like she said? He wouldn't say yes or no, they knew that much. Where the hell was Lieutenant Preece? Jacko fiddled with the radio which seemed to be dead. Corporal Box stayed on watch.

'Bother, Colour?' he asked.

'Not sure,' said Jacko. 'Trying to raise base.' The radio crackled into life. Jacko spoke quickly into it.

'Six zero bravo. Target returned home at 07:00 hours. Over.'

In the Operations Room traffic was thin in the early morning. Patrols were clattering out past the door and the men from the company would soon be deployed around the town, making their usual rounds. Major Taylor was standing at the back of the Ops Room watching as Company Sergeant-Major Gilby listened to the various calls coming in. Gilby turned to him as Jackson's message came through.

'She's just got back home, sir,' he said. 'Message from Colour-Sergeant Jackson at 07:00. Should we check with her uncle? That's where she said she was going last night.'

Major Taylor hesitated a moment, then shook his head. 'Wait,' he said, and as he said it the signaller called him over.

'Sir,' he said, 'message just coming in, sir. Bomb just gone, off, sir, at reference 239562, sir. An old bar, sir.'

Gilby had written down the figures and was already with Major Taylor checking the position on the map.

'On her route, sir. Even if she was going to her uncle,' said Gilby. Major Taylor sniffed, thought a moment.

'Recall Sergeant Bilinski,' he said to the signaller. 'Then call up Colour. I'll RV with him in twenty minutes.' He checked the map again, 'At 045357. Got that?' The signaller nodded.

Major Taylor turned to Gilby. 'You too, Sergeant-Major. I want two men left on the OP and the rest with Jackson at that location. I want two sections of Six Platoon there too. The stand-by section and Corporal Box's lads. I'll wait for you, Sergeant-Major.'

He walked quickly out of the Operations Room. Gilby raised an eyebrow at the signaller who grinned and began relaying the messages.

Gilby walked out after Major Taylor. 'Sir?' he said and Major Taylor turned from the map he was checking. 'What, exactly are we going to be doing, sir?' he asked.

'We'll put salt on her tail, Sergeant-Major. That's what we'll be doing. We will have to get an RUC man to that RV; double quick, will you?'

Gilby grinned and walked back into the Operational Room. Something to do at last. Some action at last. Not before time, in his opinion, either.

The quarry had been left unused for years. The track to it could still take four-wheel-drive vehicles even after the soaking it'd had for the past week. Colour-Sergeant Jackson and Adams walked quickly through the undergrowth covering each other as they did so. Adams nursing his SLR watched Jacko move quickly ahead of him. They leapfrogged each other from one tree to the next and eventually came out into the huge quarry. Jackson waited for Adams to join him. The quarry was deserted but it didn't do to take chances.

'Colour,' said Adams, 'what's on, then?' Jackson didn't answer. He'd left two men on the OP as ordered and got to the RV point as fast as he was able. There had been no time to ask questions and he would very certainly have had no answers if he had asked. 'Shurrup and keep your eyes open,' he said abruptly. Down the track they heard the revving engines of the Land Rovers. Jacko and Adams crouched, quietly waiting. Sergeant Bilinski was riding shotgun in the first Land Rover to come into view and behind him was another with Major Taylor and Gilby.

Adams watched as Colour, Sergeant-Major Gilby, Major Taylor and Sergeant Bilinski said good morning. He leaned back against the bole of the tree and grinned across at Twiss and Mayhoe.

'They making you work for your living, Terry?' said Twiss, grinning at the state of Adams's uniform. It was wet, covered with pine needles and dirty where he'd scuffed up some mud. Adams looked down at his clothes and smiled.

'More'n you've ever done, eh?' he said. 'Brought him along, then?' he said, pointing across at Tompkins who was standing idly by the side of the Land Rover some mud. Adams looked down at his clothes and smiled.

'More'n you've ever done, eh?' he said. 'Brought him along, then?' he said, pointing across at Tompkins who was standing idly by the side of the Land Rover.

'Scared, he is,' said Mayhoe. 'Took him out on a street patrol yesterday afternoon. And one this morning, an' all. Useless. Doesn't even know how to cross the street. He's lookin' this way and that with his eyes on bloody stalks. Shakin', weren't you, sunshine?'

The young soldier looked across at them and then walked over. The three friends watched him in silence. He stopped in front of them.

'You what?' he asked.

Adams suddenly felt sorry for him. He hadn't done anything to them and they'd spent their time taking the piss. OK, the kid was scared. Not his fault. No one could possibly train a bloke to do a street patrol. Anyway the only way to train for that is do it. No other way worth a light. No other way do you learn to believe that some bastard might, just might, take a pot-shot at you. Experience is all there is to; learn about it, he thought. He

97

nodded at Tompkins and smiled at him. 'You all right, sunshine?'

Tompkins smiled eagerly and nodded his head. 'Yeah, yeah, great. Ta.'

He reached into his pocket and offered a packet of smokes. They all took one and Tompkins was just about to light up when he noticed they'd all put their smokes into their pockets. 'Eh, what's the bloody idea?' he asked. Adams just pointed towards the group huddled over the bonnet of the Land Rover.

'Not now, sunshine. Not here. We're working, mate.' Tompkins was thick as pig shit, Adams thought, and walked away.

The map of the area was pinned down by each member of O group onto the bonnet of the Land Rover. Major Taylor made it clear that the bomb this morning seemed to be a rather pointless exercise and unlike Frank's usual modus operandi. He'd looked across at Jackson, who had nodded in agreement. On the other hand, this woman had been out on both occasions and that was a coincidence that could bear closer investigation.

'It'll be very delicate,' said Major Taylor. 'Any questions so far?' He looked around the group. They knew he wanted to ginger it up a bit and try to get some action before the company was pulled out of Ireland. They knew he wanted the feather in his cap of nobbling this bastard Frank. Major Taylor was a transparent man to those who had worked with him for long enough. Gilby and Bilinski knew very well that he would come to regard the operation as a personal matter. They knew that if they didn't nail Frank up he'd regard it as a personal failure. They rather liked him for it. He was at least human, angry, ambitious in some ways, but above all now he wanted action.

'We don't know for sure if she's on her jack, do we?' said Sergeant-Major Gilby. 'No one on watch last night. Could be anyone there, couldn't there?' He looked across at Colour-Sergeant Jackson in apparent concern. Major Taylor detected the look too.

'Our decision, a joint decision, Sergeant-Major. An error. I think we're all agreed.' He smiled at Jackson, who said nothing. Taylor wondered if perhaps his appearance of brightness was misleading, whether Jackson was, in fact, thick. It wasn't what his report had said and it wasn't what he understood from other officers. Why didn't the man say something, join in the discussion?

'We all make mistakes, sir,' said Gilby and Taylor looked at him quickly. 'That second bomb couldn't be just coincidence, could it, sir?' he asked.

Major Taylor shook his head. 'I think not.'

Colour-Sergeant Jackson leaned across the bonnet and stared down at the map for a moment. He looked up at the other men. 'She was alone. Four days and nights. So no reason to think she's not now. But we'd do well to watch it. There's buildings here and here.' He stabbed at the map. 'Out of our eyeline on the OP. Could be something there to watch for. But no signs. No extra food going in, no extra milk, no movement or lights at the back of the house at night. She was alone for the four days and nights we stayed on.'

'But you weren't on last night, Jacko. Things can change,' said Gilby.

'I think we take your point, Sergeant-Major. But Colour does know the ground, has been watching it. I want her talked to, that's all.' Major Taylor turned to Sergeant Bilinski and gave his orders. 'Just a chat, Sergeant. Just a chat, that's all. And make damn sure the back is sewn up tight. OK?'

Bilinski nodded and turned towards his patrol. Major Taylor stopped him.

'Colour,' he said, 'you'll go with them.' He saw the disappointment in Bilinski's face and smiled across at him. 'No reflection, Sergeant, but Colour's been watching the place for days. Knows it backwards, knows the exits, knows the ground. I don't want them bolting if by any chance he is there. Understand?'

Bilinski nodded and swung round to his patrol of men. He called Twiss over and the men came doubling across the quarry floor.

Major Taylor walked around to Jackson's side of the Land Rover. 'And be sure it's casual. Just a touch of pressure. Nothing heavy.' Jackson looked at Taylor a moment. 'You sure, sir?' he asked.

'Just a touch, Colour,' he repeated. 'I'm sure you'll use your judgement, won't you?' He walked across to his Land Rover and told his signaller to raise base.

Bilinski had his patrol ready and was explaining briefly what they would be doing. Jackson walked across to the Land! Rover and jerked his head at Adams, who was still leaning! against a tree. 'Join Sergeant Bilinski,' he ordered, and Adams! doubled across to the Land Rover. Jackson pulled a map of the area out of his pocket, unfolded it and spread it on the? seat. As he did so Sergeant-Major Gilby walked up to him.

'What were you at then, Tom? Putting the boot in?' asked Jacko quietly. Gilby sniffed, smiled at him and spat.

'Me?' he asked innocently. 'Not me. Just pointing out the facts, Colour-Sergeant. My job,' he said, and leaned closer to Jackson.

'Get it right, Jacko, or your chances are pudding, aren't they? Know what I mean? So gently, gently . . . very gently.'

After a moment Jackson picked up the map and walked across to Sergeant Bilinski. 'Right?' he said and Bilinski nodded. 'We'll split into three. A section to cover the back will go in first. A section to cover the front and the sides will cover us as the third group go into the house. Right? Simple, direct and no fucking around.'

The group grinned and nodded.

'Who goes in?' asked Twiss. 'Colour,' he said as an afterthought.

'Adams, Mayhoe, you, Twiss, and that lad there, what's your name?' He pointed at the young soldier just out of depot.

'Me, Colour?' he said.

'You sunshine. Name.'

'Tompkins, Colour,' the lad said.

'You'll be coming into the house. Experience for you.' They had to start some time, Jackson thought. 'You'll come, Sergeant, right?'

Bilinski was pleased. 'Right,' he said.

'Let's go then.' Jackson turned away to his Land Rover, stuffing the map back into his pocket. Gilby watched him drive out and within a few minutes there was no sound to be heard in the quarry. Gilby and Major Taylor settled down to await results. Ninety-nine per cent boredom and one per cent mind-riveting fear, as someone once described the soldier's life. Maybe, thought Gilby, maybe it is. Major Taylor sat and drummed his fingers on the armour-plating sheets that covered the back of the vehicle. He was impatient for success.

Early morning also came to Strathfelt. Along the river on the edge of the town a line of fences was strewn with advertisements and old posters. At the far end a high brick wall butted off an old terrace of houses and protected Andrews Paint Factory and Stores. It was the only bit of light industry that had survived the years of fighting and disturbance in the area. Outside the walls a number of cars were parked. Only a few places were left as the blue Ford Cortina drove slowly past the gates of the factory and eased into a space. The man who got out of the car was hardly remarkable, except for the cut of his suit, perhaps, which identified him as a townie rather than a country lad. He had a shock of black hair and sported a big black beard.

His card, which he showed to the security man at the gate, said that he worked as a buyer for a large organization in Belfast. The firm was old and the buildings confusing. It was remarkably difficult not to get lost at times, even if you knew the place well.

The man was not about the place for long, however, and he walked casually away down the road, past the cars parked beside the wall and close to the terrace of houses. Indeed, he walked straight past the blue Ford Cortina - hadn't he driven up in that car not an hour since? But then perhaps he just wanted to stretch his legs.

He walked on and round the corner, down towards river crossing and away from the little town.

Chapter Six

That was the day Tompkins got hit. They'd all been in the area and no one had stopped Tompkins. Adams might have, Major Taylor would have if he'd seen the lad, Twiss would have if the silly bastard wasn't going to get him killed too, and Mayhoe would have, except that he was busy finding the biggest bomb he ever wanted to see.

Jacko sat back in the armchair and looked across at Mary's father as he poured another nightcap. The women had gone upstairs to bed and left them to it. Leave hadn't been too much of a strain. Well, not more than usual. His mother-in-law had twittered on a bit and Mr Barker seemed to think he knew what to do in Northern Ireland, like everyone else seemed to know except me, thought Jacko. He hadn't talked about it, hadn't wanted to and had refused to be drawn. It was all so stupid when kids like that got themselves killed for no good reason. OK, an old woman refused to move out of her house. OK, Tompkins wasn't experienced. All true, but he'd still got himself blown to bits.

'You're very quiet, Jack,' said his father-in-law, handing him a large whisky. 'Have been since you came here.'

'Yes,' Jacko agreed. 'Sorry.'

The old man settled into his chair. He quite liked Mary's husband, though he still hadn't got used to the idea that they seemed to have a good marriage and the kids were polite and quiet about the place. Be thankful for small mercies. He looked across at Jack, who was sipping his scotch. 'That lad. The one who got himself killed.' Jacko had mentioned him in passing and had dropped the subject.

'A shame, that.' Jacko said nothing. I'm sorry about it. But it shows . . . They're ruthless. You've got to use the same tactics back.'

Jacko just stared at him. The old boy didn't know what he was talking about. To use those sort of tactics you've got to hate a great deal and Jacko didn't hate them. He hated being there but he didn't hate the people as much as those bombers seemed to.

'I don't want to talk about him,' he said and put down his drink. 'He was stupid, irresponsible. He could've killed the lot of us. It was lucky he didn't. A silly, silly bastard.'

'Brave, would you say?' asked the old man and Jacko shook his head.

'I don't know about that. He didn't do the job right, that's all I know. And he's dead and gone and no bloody use to man nor beast, is he?'

The old man was shocked by Jacko's attitude. He found it hard to believe that any man could be so detached about it.

'That's very cold, Jack,' he said.

Jacko put his glass down and said nothing for a moment. Then, 'Listen, you say you're sorry. You didn't know him. You don't know any of them out there, do you? It's changed, Mr Barker, since your day. All right, the army was one thing during the war. It's not the same now. It's highly trained, it uses all the mechanical aids it can lay its hands on, it moves fast and it has good weapons. I'll tell you, only one thing has stayed the same. It takes men to do it, men to use the weapons, drive the trucks, check the surveillance gear. And they get killed. It's the chance you take. We could all be sitting on our arses in an office pushing pens but we're not. Half the lads who join, join because there's not much else. We've a glut of recruits just now. We're even fussy about who we take in and who we don't. They have to be able to read and write. It's a step in the right direction, maybe. They can think and they can answer for themselves. But they don't change the score in Ireland because we are one step behind the politicos. Any other army in the world would have gone through that whole community like knives through butter and they'd have been lucky to come out the other end with a civilian population. We haven't done that, have we?'

'And what would happen, Jack?' asked the old man quietly. Jacko looked at him helplessly and shook his head.

'I don't know. All I know is we lost a little lad just out of depot, and we buried him there because he didn't have anyone to send the bits to here, and we all felt sick and angry and there's plenty of men in the Wessex Rangers who wanted to stay and nail up the bastard responsible. And I don't want to talk about it any more. OK?'

The old man sighed, pushed the bottle of whisky closer to Jack and got up. I'll go to bed, I think, Jack. Put the light out, will you, when you come up ?'

He walked to the door and looked back as Jacko poured another drink.

'I'm sorry, Jacko,' he said and walked out. Jacko drank down the whisky in one. That bastard Ireland. All that hate and anger and a young lad driving a car for all the right reasons blown to fuck. The only whole bit they'd found was a hand on the steering wheel. Jacko poured another drink.

It was the day after the pub blast. In the OP at the edge of the trees Corporal Box stared down at the house through his binoculars. He turned to the signaller lying next to him in the wet.

'It's like a bloody morgue down there. When the hell are they moving in ?'

The signaller pointed and Box turned to look again. Behind the house he saw a man run across a gap in the hedge, wait and cover the next man. A section of soldiers moved slowly to take up position behind the buildings to

105

the left of the yard. From there they could cover all exits from the back of the house. As he watched a second section moved from their Land Rovers down the track and fanned out to cover the front. Overhead a Gazelle spotter-helicopter swooped, apparently aimlessly, out of the sky across the farm. Box grinned. Major Taylor was taking no chances with this one, he thought.

In the house the woman heard the helicopter and went to the window of her living-room to see what it was. As she looked out she saw a section of soldiers moving into position down the track to the house and a Land Rover driving slowly into the yard, wheeling to a stop just beyond the front door. She watched as six men got out of the Land Rover. She noted the name of the regiment without much interest. Just so long as it wasn't the Paras she didn't feel too scared. She'd been told that they came in boot first and questions after. She'd seen friends of hers with bleeding heads and broken ribs after they'd been kicked and hit with staves. Frank called it 'Asking questions.' And she knew that worse had happened in the quiet rooms about Belfast and Lismore. It was all part of the game, according to Frank. She'd seen him when he first came away from one of those sessions and had been horrified. It was in a way that that had turned her from a sympathizer into an active helper. 'While those bastards are here,' he'd said, 'there will be no justice, no honest settlement and we have to fight them as the arm of a system that has kept ordinary people poor for four hundred years. Not Catholics and Protestants, this isn't. This is just the poor against the others. Don't kid yourself, Marie,' he'd say. 'This is the capitalists struggling for survival and we'll not let them.' Much of what they'd talked about she hadn't understood. Often he'd stopped talking to her because he knew she wasn't able to follow his argument, but always she stayed with him because he was saying something that she felt in her bones was right. They'd been confused by the sectarian struggle and that was a part of the overall plot. 'To hell with God and religion and all that opiate,' he'd shout when he was angry. 'To hell with that cant. We want a better Ireland for all the people all of the time. And without the English Parliament or their army or any of it.'

His friends in the South regarded him with a mixture of fear and respect. They admired his skill with bits of metal, fertilizers, explosives and other chemicals. He seemed to be able to make an explosion with anything at all. And he enjoyed his work. She was glad that he wasn't here now and that there was nothing to link him with the farmhouse. The last time he'd been here was over a year back and since then they'd met in private houses, or occasionally in clubs outside the main towns. As she watched the soldiers group around the Land Rover a civilian car raced up the drive and a member of the RUC got out and walked across to the soldiers. It's a search then, she thought. Why the hell me? How the hell have they tied me in? 'Be the innocent and smile with your heart at the murdering fuckers' Frank had always said. 'Never admit a thing and never refuse them permission to search, for they'll search anyway, whatever you say, and if you've said no, you've something to hide and that's when they find something. Something, as likely as not, they've put there themselves. So say yes sir, no sir, and smile all the time.'

The woman dropped the corner of the curtain and turned back into the room. There was little of comfort about the place. Since she lived alone and wasn't too fussy the place was a tip. Automatically, like any woman, she began to tidy around. She stopped and began to laugh. 'Jesus Mary, what am I doing that for? So's a muddy soldier won't think I'm a slut.' She threw down the newspaper she'd picked up. The door was knocked once and then twice more. She looked at herself in the mirror, pushed a strand of hair back into place and decided she looked a bit too tired. Some early nights now and no more jaunting about the country for a bit. Not if they were getting this close. She'd have to get a message to Frank, warn him they were watching her. That wasn't going to be easy. They knocked on the door again.

Bilinski checked his rifle and his patrol did the same. He looked across at Jackson who had just knocked at the door.

'Gently, gently, Jacko,' he said quietly. These were always the bad moments. Once the door was open they would know if there was someone inside. They'd be met either with a rapid-fire fusillade down the hall, and they made sitting ducks for that, or they'd tell from the fear in the eyes of the woman when she answered. Jackson turned to the tall constable who'd arrived just in time. 'You know what we want?' he asked and the green-uniformed man nodded.

'A look around, I was told. Leave it to me.'

She was taking her time about answering and Colour-Sergeant Jackson was beginning to wonder if the bird had flown. Hanging about waiting for the RUC always made him edgy. Why the hell they couldn't just get on with the job instead of pretending they needed the constabulary to hold their hands he didn't really know. Support for the forces of law and order. Jesus! They were the forces of law and order. The constable looked at the soldier and the constable's mouth was a thin line. He's scared, thought Jacko. Still, to tell the truth, I'm not exactly liking this meself. He banged the door again and it immediately swung open.

The woman looked up at the soldiers standing in the doorway. Bilinski, with his back to her and covering the front bay window, another two soldiers facing up the drive and this tall, dark one with such dead eyes looking directly at her. He'd his gun in the crook of his arm and he only

108

flicked a glance at her before he looked past her down the hall to the stairs at the end. The constable did the talking. 'Routine, missus. I'd like a word.'

She glanced at him once and then didn't bother to look again. 'And your friends?' she asked, staring at the colour-sergeant.

'And them,' said the constable.

The soldier didn't do more than glance at her when she spoke. She was afraid all right but was smiling just like Frank had always said.

'It's an awful lot of grown men to hold your hand, mister,' she mocked the constable. 'And me on me own too. Don't they say there's safety in numbers, Sergeant?'

'Yes, ma'am. Just a word or two. No more,' said Jacko. She was a very attractive woman. Much prettier than the photograph had shown. She looked tired about the eyes but her mouth was firm and strong and her hair that jet-black some of these girls seemed to have. He caught her watching him as he looked her over.

'Sure I'm glad there's so many then,' she said, smiling. 'You'd best come in. I've a kettle boiling.' And she turned her back on the group at the door and walked down the hallway, past the bottom of the stairs and into the kitchen. Behind her the section came in fast. She turned back to watch them. The sergeant went straight to the front living-room, door open and then fast in with gun at the ready. The other sergeant followed him as the black one was half-way up the stairs checking the landing, and the youngest one was standing cover at the open front door. One of the soldiers was walking down towards her as she watched.

'All right, Johnny?' he asked the blackie on the stairs.

'All right,' said the soldier.

She waited until the young soldier was near her. Adams smiled at her almost apologetically. He waited a pace or two from her.

109

'A talk was it, or a search?' she asked him. He shrugged and gestured to the kitchen with his gun.

'You had a kettle on. Is there tea in the pot?' he said, and she turned quietly away down the dark corridor that led to the back kitchen. He followed her at a distance until they got close to the door of the kitchen and then he was very close behind her. She opened the door and walked into the kitchen. He looked around fast. The room was empty.

'See,' she said. 'Not a bogey man in sight, soldier.'

'Best to be sure, isn't it?' he said. He noticed the teapot. 'Be a help, that would, love,' he said.

'I can make it meself, soldier. I don't need help. I've had practice enough.' She didn't want him in her kitchen. She'd never had the soldiers over her place and already she was beginning not to like it. They walked in, took over, looked into things, checked things and all the time not interested in you but more in something else. Secrets, perhaps. If you had any.

'Nice place,' said the soldier, looking around the large kitchen.

'Yes,' she said and warmed the teapot with water from the kettle.

'On your own, are you?' he asked. She walked across to a cupboard and took out the tea caddy. She put three spoonsful into the pot and a half one for luck.

'Lucky,' he said when she didn't answer, 'with all this to yourself. Back home my missus has to live with mum and dad. No space.'

He seemed a nice enough lad. All right, you couldn't trust them but he did seem nice and she didn't want them all pawing over her things.

'Will they be looking the house over just to be checking? Is that what a little chat is?' she asked. The soldier smiled at her and picked up a biscuit from a plate. He looked for permission and she nodded.

'You've nothing to worry about. No one's going to touch anything, madam,' he said. He rested the butt of his SLR on the kitchen table as he broke the biscuit and ate it slowly. 'I've heard it before, soldier. Doors kicked in, they say, and furniture broken. It's happened.'

He looked at her quite deadpan and nodded. 'Yeah,' he said, 'not me. Kettle.' He pointed at the plume of steam rising from the kettle.

Tompkins stood at the open front door of the farmhouse. Outside he could see Three Section deployed along the lane and across the front of the house. He leaned against the wall and held his rifle awkwardly, ready for use. Behind him, in the front living-room, he could hear the quiet voices of Colour-Sergeant Jackson and the RUC constable. Sergeant Bilinski had already been upstairs with that blackie, Mayhoe, and checked the bedrooms for anyone hidden there. They'd drawn a blank. Mayhoe waited at the door of the living-room with his rifle casually held under one arm. The woman came along the passage ahead of Adams and walked into the living-room, the teapot on a tray with mugs and milk and sugar. She looked around the room and at the men cluttering it up.

'Nice of you,' said the tall sergeant as she poured mugs of tea for them.

'Not much choice, have I?' she said bitterly. Frank had always warned her never to provoke them and to stay neutral if they ever came to search. It wasn't as easy as he seemed to think. This was her home these soldiers were standing in. This was her mess in the living-room. She had a right, surely, to peace and security in her own home? What damned right did they have to go about scaring innocent women? She stopped in her train of thought for a moment. Innocent? Well, as far as they knew she was. She took up the sugar basin. 'Sugar all round?' she asked.

'Thanks,' said the sergeant. 'Adams, make sure Tompkins and Mayhoe get some, OK?' The nice lad

111

who'd followed her into the kitchen nodded and took his mug of tea from her.

'There's plenty wouldn't do this,' said the colour-sergeant. 'Their own reasons, I suppose.' He smiled at her and she knew she'd have to be on her guard. He'd a way with him, this one, and he knew it as well as she did. He'd had a time with the women, this one, and was used to charming them off trees. Well, not Marie, she thought.

'Yes,' she said shortly. 'Maybe they have.'

'You on your own here? It's a big place,' said the RUC constable. She watched as the colour-sergeant glanced irritably at the constable. There wasn't a lot of love lost between these two, she thought. It'll maybe be something to use later.

'The soldier already checked that. I told him.' She looked at Adams, who nodded a confirmation at the colour-sergeant. For a moment they sat silently and sipped their tea.

'What did you want to talk about then?' she asked eventually. It wasn't easy with five soldiers in your living-room to stay detached. They seemed to have all the time in the world and were certainly in no hurry to ask their questions and go. She suddenly thought, what if Frank decided to come? What if he thinks it's all clear, wants to come over and see me? Surely he'd have sense enough to check first? He'd see the soldiers around the house, wouldn't he?'

'When did you last see Frank?' asked the tall sergeant casually as he put down his mug of tea. She was surprised at the directness of the question and frightened by it.

'Who?' she said.

The colour-sergeant stood straighter now and faced her. The other soldiers were ranged around the room casually, almost as if they were bored spectators of what was going to happen. She suddenly felt afraid. They were so calm, so cold, so disinterested, and she knew of

112

instances before when in soldiers had come into places like this determined to find answers, whatever they might be.

'You know who,' said the colour-sergeant and he was smiling at her. She didn't understand it. 'When did you last see him?'

'He's inside, isn't he?' said Marie. She didn't know how much the soldier knew. She didn't even know they'd connected her with Frank and she didn't know yet that they knew him to be a bomb maker. It wasn't going to be easy for her and this tall soldier seemed to grow colder by the second. 'He's out now,' said the colour-sergeant gently. She turned away from him and looked across the room at the soldier, Adams. He stared at her without a sign of expression in his face. The other soldier staring out of the window looked at her once, hitched his gun to a more comfortable position and turned back to stare out of the window. She shook her head.

'I haven't seen him,' she said.

The tall sergeant stepped closer to her and she backed away automatically. I'm not going to touch you, madam,' he said. 'He's been seen. You and Frank were a pigeon pair.'

She shook her head again. No one knew about them. No one who wasn't family or close friend. So who'd been talking? 'I don't know what you mean,' she said. 'Nothing to do with me, Sergeant, what he does.'

The sergeant sighed and looked across at Adams. 'What time did she leave the house last night?'

Adams looked without interest at her. 'You left at ten yesterday morning. Came back at eleven thirty.' She said nothing.

'True,' the sergeant snapped. She jerked round to look back at him as Adams went on.

'You also came back to the house this morning at seven. Where had you been? Shopping?'

'I went to see my uncle. I went through his road

113

block.' She suddenly recognized Sergeant Bilinski. 'He stopped me. I told him.'

'Yes,' said the colour-sergeant. 'You told him. Where else had you been?'

'Out. It was a fine morning. I went out,' she said.

'Where?' asked the sergeant.

She began to bluster. 'I don't see what this . . .' The sergeant turned away from her and walked past the RUC constable, who hadn't taken his eyes off her the whole time. Jacko didn't want this to go too far. He wanted no reason for lifting her yet. They could do that any time. He just wanted her afraid and anxious to make a move. They needed a lead to that bloody bomber and she was the only hope they had.

'You don't have to tell us, missus,' he said and watched the relief spread across her face. 'Forget it just now. Is there another cup in the pot?'

She was angry now. 'What the hell d'you want?' she demanded. She pushed a strand of hair back into place and her pale face was twisted with anger and fear. Jacko knew the signs and he knew that she was scared sick. Go easy was the name of the game. He smiled a touch.

'Told you when we came in. A chat, and a cuppa. Very welcome.' He bent and poured himself more tea. 'You don't mind, do you?' he asked.

'You've no right. Not to do this. You know that,' she said. And he looked at her for a moment and then glanced across at the constable.

'He's with us. RUC. It's legal enough,' he said. 'More than you can say about Frank. But we're not going to talk about that, are we? Not yet. Eh?'

The soldier by the window had turned now and was staring at her openly. He fingered the trigger guard of his gun and smiled suddenly at a thought. She watched him and wished he'd say something, anything. He just stared at her.

114

She turned back to the colour-sergeant and he said nothing while he drank his tea. The soldier by the door watched her for a moment and then walked out of the room. May hoe came in and found a mug poured ready for him. He brushed past the woman, who instinctively drew back. He looked at her for a moment and then stepped across to the soldier in the bay window.

The mirror on the wall over the fireplace reflected them all. For a moment she caught herself fixed in the mirror and noticed that she was looking anything but easy. The smile no longer flashed across her face. She felt suddenly tired and sick.

'If you don't believe me,' she said eventually, 'look around, check.'

Colour-Sergeant Jackson nodded once, jerked his head at the blackie and the other sergeant. They walked straight out of the room past her and past the RUC constable. No one said anything. She stepped one pace towards the door and then stopped where she was. The young soldier from the kitchen walked back into the room and shut the door.

She looked from him to the RUC man and neither of them appeared to her to have any feelings showing in their eyes. She was afraid now. Adams sat down on an upright chair with his gun between his knees and stared up at her. She watched him, afraid to move. She sniffed with fear, pushed her hand through her hair and then put both hands together. She could feel them both beginning to shake. Outside the room she could hear the thud of doors being wrenched open, the squeak of drawers and the rattle of cupboard doors being opened.

'It's not right,' she said weakly. Adams smiled at her. And stared across the foresight of his SLR.

'Missus,' he said, 'don't make trouble with him. Colour-Sergeant is bad news. We know about Frank and we know about you, see? You'd do yourself a bit of good if you just opened up a bit. See?' He was still smiling. She hesitated and then walked across to the windows. She lifted the net curtains and looked out again. It was still and quiet out there. The soldiers were still in their vehicles. That'd warn Frank off if he did come. It wasn't fair. Not to have this. He hadn't told her it'd be like this. Just smile and they'll go away. No bother, my darling, he used to say. He didn't know. Didn't know what it was like to have their filthy boots all over the place and blackies looking through your things and all. Frank wouldn't want to wash every damn thing they might have touched because he felt soiled by it all. They just come in so quiet, so calm, chat, chat, cup of tea, have a look round, and on their way and they leave behind their filth. She was trying hard not to cry. She shook her head.

The soldier didn't raise his voice. He didn't even move. It was as if he was thinking through the problem from her point of view.

Adams looked across at Twiss standing still by the window. He knew what Twiss wanted to do and he knew that had he been alone with her, or with her and Adams without Colour and the rest, then this woman would've told them anything and everything. Twiss had a streak of the bastard in him that made him dangerous. Leave him alone and this woman would be begging to tell them everything they wanted to hear. If Twiss threatened to do something then you knew he'd do it. Twiss glanced across at Adams and sneered. He's bothered, thought Twiss. Bothered about her, the bitch. She knows what she's doing, she blew Gaddy up, could've killed him and the rest, the cow. And what are we doing pansying about in her fucking house? I'd rip the bastard place shred from fucking shred, me. I'd have her, I'd smash her if I could. Just let them get out and leave it to me. He slammed the rifle butt against the wooden window frame in frustration.

The woman looked round sharply at the noise. She was afraid of that one by the window. He'd not smiled nor

116

drunk his tea nor done anything but stare at her with his cold, piggy eyes. He looked pale and the lines around his eyes were lines of tiredness, but she could see the cruelty in him and she was afraid that the other one would go out. She turned to Adams.

'I don't know what you all want,' she said. Adams stepped closer to her. He spoke quietly.

'Look,' he said. 'No one would point the finger. No one need to know. Call us. I'll give you a number.' He scribbled a number on a pad he took from his pocket and handed it to her. She didn't take it so he put the sheet of paper on the table by the teapot. 'Just call us, love. It'd be best, you know.' He smiled at her and she didn't know what to do or say. 'He's dangerous, you know, Frank. Dangerous to himself. He could kill himself. Maybe.'

'I haven't seen him. Not a sign. I told you.' She knew he didn't believe her. He pointed at the paper. 'In case you remember then. Eh?' he said. 'You're lucky, you know.' She didn't understand him. He was so quiet and gentle. He wasn't what she'd expected. The one by the window, he was, and the others. Stamping about, checking, looking through you as if you were vermin. Frank was right about them, but this man, Adams, he wasn't the same. He seemed soft in a way. She looked up as the door of the room opened and the whey-faced soldier from the hall came in. He was only a kid and seemed to be more afraid than anything else. Adams turned sharply. 'What the hell d'you want?' he barked. Tompkins hesitated.

'I thought maybe a cuppa . . .'

'You left the fucking front door, did you?' Tompkins turned quickly and closed the door as he went out.

Adams shook his head at Twiss. 'Stupid twat,' said Twiss. 'A bloody liability, the wet-arsed berk.' Twiss went back to watching from the window. Adams looked at her and she turned away and stared at the mirror on the wall.

'You're lucky,' Adams repeated. She didn't turn

117

round.

'You said so. Why?' she asked.

'Having a place like this. Quiet. Peaceful sort of a place. And big enough. I've got a place. Not enough room to swing a cat.' She turned round to face him again. He was looking around the room. 'The wife hates it,' he went on. She sat down in the armchair near the fire. The one Frank had always used. His chair, he'd called it when he'd lived there. She took up the newspaper from its arm and threw it aside. 'Is she with you? Here?'

Adams shook his head. 'No, she didn't want to. It's the job, isn't it? Not safe.'

She began to laugh and then stopped abruptly. 'The job,' she said bitterly. 'Your job. Chasing women and kids. That.'

He shrugged and turned away from her. 'If you say so,' he said and she came out of her chair fast. He turned as she moved and she realized that he had never been as relaxed as she thought, that he had never for a moment forgotten what he was doing and what she might just possibly do. She flicked a glance across the room and found that the soldier was leaning back against the centre of the bay window with his gun at the ready all right. For a moment they stood quite still. The flare of anger died away and Marie began to sob. The two soldiers watched her in silence

'That's what it is, though, isn't it? You solving anything here, are you? With that?' She pointed blindly at the SLR Adams now had carelessly aimed at her body. He moved the gun aside, yet he still didn't raise his voice.

'I don't know,' he said. 'It's my job. What's your friend Frank solving with his bombs? What's he solve with them?' Adams asked her gently. And suddenly she realized what he'd been doing all the time he'd been in the room. This gentle, quiet, sympathetic young boy had been fooling with her. Everything she'd said or not said he'd been

118

pushing and angling for. The softness was a delusion or he wouldn't be here at all, the gentleness a trap to ease her into trusting him, the sympathy as synthetic and phoney as the sorrow she was supposed to have felt for her dead mother when she finally let go her grip on living.

This young man was as much a betrayer and as devious as Frank had warned her they might be. What she hadn't been prepared for was the soft touch. The stories about their violence, their vandalism, their barbarity, the torture and the interrogations had passed long since into the mythology of the struggle and it was these things she had always heard from Frank. He had it wrong. They were more subtle than that now and doubly dangerous. Marie lifted her head and looked Adams in the face as he repeated his question.

'What's he solving anyway? Tell me.'

'Ask him,' she said. 'He knows.' And she walked quickly away from him as he offered her a cigarette from his packet. She leaned with her back to the wall and stared back at him defiantly. The anger had gone now, and determination and a cold certainty that this time they would get nothing more from her, whatever they might try, had replaced it.

She could feel the cold stone wall behind her through the skin of plaster and she could remember the arguments and bickering of her mother and father that had occupied the whole of their married life since she could remember. They had no sons to work the pitiful land and if they had had sons, those sons would have left for England or the States or wherever their chances were equal to those of the other people about them. Here in this bleak place was no comfort, no hope, nor even the possibility of earning more than a pittance of a living, and her bitterness rose up almost to choke her.

Adams looked across at Twiss and grinned. Twiss sniffed and rubbed his nose with the back of his hand.

'She's a bright one,' he said and ran a finger round his throat as the women did to them every day they took a patrol through the streets.

'You lot,' he said. 'You don't deserve us. You deserve some bastard to come along and put a bomb under here of a night and blow the whole fucking shebang up in the air. That'd be good for you, darling.' Twiss didn't raise his voice and she didn't even look across at him. No one spoke now until the door opened again and Adams turned to check it while Twiss watched the woman on the other side of the room. Colour-Sergeant Jackson walked into the room with the rest of the section. Jacko looked at Adams and the cold-eyed Twiss and the two men lowered their rifles. Jacko walked across to the woman, who stared bleakly up at him.

'Thanks for the tea. We won't bother you any more,' he said.

'What did I tell you? Nothing was there. Nothing at all.'

Jackson smiled at her and shrugged. 'Just a routine chat, madam,' he said.

The section had lined up by the door and Jacko walked across to them. The RUC constable stood in the doorway itself. Jacko turned back to the woman. 'Please,' he said. 'This is as much for your good as mine.'

She moved across to the soldiers and didn't look at them. She was puzzled. What were they going to do now? The sergeant stepped up to the colour-sergeant and ran his hands quickly and expertly down his body. He patted each pocket, checked that the bulge in the top jacket pocket was a clip of ammunition and then the colour-sergeant did the same to him. The body search was carried through quickly and efficiently by the colour-sergeant.

'Just to make sure, madam. Don't want you rushing off to the local constabulary and claiming we stole the family silver, do we?' He smiled at her.

He checked Twiss last and then nodded to Sergeant Bilinski. 'Right, Sergeant. That's that, I think.' The soldiers moved quickly out of the front room and down the hallway to the door. She watched them leave without moving from the room. The young soldier, Tompkins, went past her without looking across at her. 'Thanks,' he said and moved out past the colour-sergeant.

She looked again at the tall, dark man who hesitated a moment by the door. 'You've got the Boys Brigade out, have you?' she said bitterly. The colour-sergeant smiled and nodded.

'You could say that. Tarrah. Thanks for the tea.' He walked quietly into the hall, closing the door behind him.

They'd done the house over thoroughly. Every room checked, every drawer looked into. Jackson knew they'd no chance of finding anything and he didn't really want to find anything either, but he had to make the visit look authentic. Under no circumstances had he wanted to bring her in and he knew damned well that Major Taylor would have had his balls if he had done so. He stood for a moment in the hall.

The woman was scared but she'd got a lot of fight in her. If she hadn't been carrying for that bloody bomb maker Jacko knew he'd have found a sneaking admiration for her. She seemed so bloody lonely up here. The large bed was very obviously meant to be slept in by two and nothing provided evidence of there ever being anyone in the house except her. What the hell was an attractive woman doing mixed up with a cold-blooded bastard who'd blow anyone or anything to bits if it just happened to get in the way?

'Jacko.' Sergeant Bilinski was waiting in the doorway.

'Ready.' Jacko walked quickly out past him and across to the revving Land Rover. He swung into the passenger seat while Sergeant Bilinski climbed into the back .'On your way,' he said to the driver and the Land

Rover turned fast across the yard and away from the farmhouse.

Marie walked away from the bay window and shivered. It wasn't cold and people said you shiver when a goose steps on your grave. She noticed the piece of paper that Adams had scrawled a number on. Slowly, methodically and without even looking at it, she tore the paper to shreds. She walked out of the living-room and slowly up the stairs to see what they had done.

In her bedroom the wardrobe doors hung open and the drawers in the dressing-table, the contents spilled all over the bed. The bed cover had been pulled back and she saw that and began to cry. To search the bed, to look for evidence in a bed to see if Frank had been in touch, been here, slept with her. He hadn't slept with her for so long now she had almost forgotten what it was like. 'We've got work to do, Marie,' he'd say. 'Work.'

Chapter Seven

Adams and Tsai sat in the Railwaymen's Arms on the last night of leave. It hadn't been a bed of roses and after the first afternoon he'd hardly spoken to his mum and dad. The two of them hadn't said much to each other throughout the last evening. Leave had been a failure in other ways too, and Terry Adams didn't know how to talk about that.

He'd promised to try and get a quarter when he went back to Tidworth. He'd promised that he wouldn't make her stay much longer in Sebastopol Street with his mum and dad. He would find a quarter. He had no idea how he'd manage to pay for it but he'd have to until he found her a place on the camp.

He looked across at her and remembered the sickening panic of his return home, the reluctance he had felt as he left Twiss and Mayhoe on that afternoon at Tidworth two weeks ago. As he had walked across to his motorbike he had turned to see them standing on the balcony outside barrack room A, Twiss dressed in his new suit and Mayhoe grinning with pleasure at the thought of seeing his girl again.

Adams had kicked the motorcycle into life, glad, at least, of the chance of an hour or two on his own. The sun was sinking lower in the sky as he had made the journey north to Swindon.

He had swung his Norton 1000cc through the right-hander, missed a couple of school kids on bikes and turned left along the terrace of houses. Sebastopol Street, Swindon, was home for Adams. He had gentled back the accelerator and the engine had begun to idle.

There had been no one in the street and although the afternoon wasn't yet over, the street was in shadow. The flat frontages were an apoplectic red brick and the window frames and doors the dull grey or green that local authorities painted their worst properties, when they bothered to paint them at all.

For a moment he'd remembered the bright yellows and greens, the brilliant reds and oranges of the flowers and trees in Malaya, the rich smell of the earth and the shouts of excited kids flying their kites beyond the village in the fields. Tsai had left all that to come here to the dullness and the grey faces and the lethargy of England. She had left behind the promise of work as a teacher in the little village school. She had left behind the laughter in her home and come to this drab relic of Victorian enterprise. She had been so eager to come and to meet his mother and father, so sure that they would be happy to see her for the first time, so anxious to make the right impression on them. She always reminded him of the respect that is due to the old and to parents.

Adams swung the bike to the kerb, revved it once and switched off. He sat a moment and stared along the street to the corner patch of the waste ground where he and his mates had played soldiers as kids. It was dirtier now and covered with the rubbish the collectors forgot or refused to take.

He took off his crash helmet, swung his leather-clad leg over the bike and stepped reluctantly along the alleyway at the side of the house. It all seemed so much smaller than it had once been.

In the kitchen Mrs Adams was making tea. She and her husband had a routine and nothing changed it. That girl had tried to change things but they'd soon sorted her out. 'Damn foreigner, telling us in our own house. No idea what Terry was up to. Stupid . . . stupid . . .'

The back door banged open and she looked up. Terry stood in the doorway.

'You're back then,' she said and didn't move towards

124

him. They'd never bothered with kissing and things in their family. He walked quietly into the kitchen and put his crash helmet on the chair by the stove.

'Where is she?' he asked. She looked at him, appearing not to understand. 'Where is she?' he repeated and stepped closer to her. He seemed to her to be angry, to be ready even to hit her. She stepped away from him.

'Out,' she said. He walked straight past her into the living-room where his father half sat, half sprawled looking at the television in the corner. The curtain was drawn to prevent the afternoon light spoiling the picture. The three o'clock race was just ending. Terry walked in, switched it off and only then did his father look up.

'What's up, our Terry?' he asked plaintively.

'Where's Tsai?' he said again. 'Where the hell is she?' Behind him his mother had come in and he looked from one to the other. They glanced at each other and then his father shrugged.

'Out,' he said. Terry knew that Tsai was unhappy, knew his mother and father had not made it easy for her.

'Where?' he asked. 'Where did she go?'

'I don't know and I don't care,' said his mother and he turned fast to her, a fist raised. 'I mean it. I mean it. No use to man nor beast. Moping about all the time. No better than she should have been. Terry!' she screamed as he went out and thundered up the stairs into the front room that was theirs. He crashed through the door and stopped dead. The room was empty.

Slowly he turned and walked down the stairs. He went back into the living-room where his father had already turned the television back on. He walked across the room and ripped the plug from the wall as his mother and father watched him. Quite suddenly they were afraid of him. Since he'd been away he'd changed and they had reason to be afraid.

'Why?' he asked. 'Why can't you accept her?'

125

'I dunno what you had to do it for, Terry. Plenty of nice girls round here. Better than her sort. Took her off of a Malayan street, I suppose, and then she'd got you. Guilty, were you, and she just played up to it?' His mother whined out her futile justifications. 'I didn't want you to join. Nor your dad, did you, dad?' Astonished to be asked anything the older man could only nod blankly and then after a moment he spoke.

'I had a go in the army, son. I told you. A real go. Real war. None of your playing games around the place. Waste of taxpayers' money, all of it, if you ask me. I told you, I'd get you a job down the works. You'd've been all right down there. All right.' He had never talked for so long together since Terry had known him. Terry turned back to his mother.

'You hate her,' shouted Terry. 'She told me. You on at her all the time, on and on and on and not helping her. A foreign kid trying to find things out and all you could do was complain. You've done that all your fucking life, haven't you?'

Terry walked out of the room fast, through the mean kitchen, picking up his white crash helmet and out into the fresh air again. Inside they were already shouting at each other. Nothing had changed at home, Terry thought.

He almost envied that poor bastard Tompkins, who hadn't got any parents to collect the bits. He'd been spared the shrieking and rows and moaning and nagging and all that bleating. And the sack they'd had to gather the bits up in had been put away decent and clean and no fussing.

The stupid, bloody idiot kid, Adams thought. Christ! I hardly knew him from Adam and I can't forget watching him crawl across the dead ground and not knowing what he was doing and then suddenly he was up like a ferret and away across the open space and into the car and driving it. Jesus God! what a bastard, and not a chance to stop him. Adams was still angry with himself. He'd been the last

126

bloke to talk to Tompkins and he'd told him he was a stupid fucker and to grow up. And then he'd done that. OK, the sergeant-major thought he was a bloody fool, useless. Adams had heard him say that. Jackson thought the same, probably, and Twiss wouldn't even remember the name, but he'd been with the kid when they tried to get the old woman out of her house. The stubborn old woman had caused him to get it. She'd never know, maybe, but it was her fault too. In a way. And he drove the car five hundred yards, with soldiers and vehicles scattering, before it began to blow to bits and screaming, jagged lumps of metal and soft tatters of flesh were flying about the street of that mean little town. And he'd gone just like that. A couple of seconds for the first explosion, then the petrol tank, and then a second explosion larger than the first. It was one of Frank's bombs OK, with the secondary device on a delay so that the disposal man would make the mistake of thinking he'd cracked it before he got his. Tompkins got the lot and they'd all come home and been told what a fine job they'd all done and how Major Taylor appreciated the back-up and nothing said about Tompkins because he was only a buckshee private and he was dead and in bits in a sack in the ground. 'Fuck it all!' yelled Adams as he pounded the bike looking for his wife. 'Fuck it all!'

In the quarry Major Taylor and Sergeant-Major Gilby waited for the search patrol to report back from their search of the woman's house. Major Taylor walked backwards and forwards across the uneven and overgrown floor of the quarry and didn't look across at the sergeant-major as he sat quietly in the front seat of the Land Rover.

Gilby wanted a cigarette and he didn't have any on him. He hated sitting about when something was happening, even if it was only 'salting the tail of the bait' as the company commander put it. He hoped Jacko would have more sense than to push her too hard. They wanted no complaints when they came out of the Province. He'd seen enough of the trouble that sort of thing made. Enquiries, second enquiries, reports, bumph and more bumph, and as often as not it was impossible to come to any conclusions one way or the other. Some of these people, Gilby thought bitterly, just want to make the job harder and to cause trouble. Even the people who the army was supposed to be protecting didn't give you a. thank you for the work done or the risks taken.

Gilby grinned to himself.

'Penny for them, Sergeant-Major,' said the company commander as he stopped his pacing beside the Land Rover.

'Sir?'

'You were grinning like a cat with cream,' said the major. Gilby wondered for a moment if he should tell this abrupt man what he had been thinking but decided that the cynicism he had about their role wasn't something Major Taylor would take kindly to.

'Nothing, sir. Just thinking about leave, sir. That's all.'

'Don't,' said Major Taylor sharply and Gilby was surprised at his tone. 'We get this damned bomber first. Don't you get days-to-do happy as well, Sergeant-Major. Won't do.' And the major resumed pacing. Gilby watched him for a moment and then sat back in the seat and waited.

He knew what his leave would be, anyway. He'd find some pub, stay bed and breakfast and itch to get back to barracks. He'd come back to listen to all the stories in the mess about the good times everyone had had and he'd contribute his share of the stories. Had to keep up the image.

He stared up at the cliff of the quarry. Water ran down the face and small bushes clung to the sides of the rock with a tenacity for life that the sergeant-major marvelled at. It seemed suddenly to him that the only thing that willingly gave up life, and did so wantonly, was man.

128

He'd seen it happen in so many places and under so many different circumstances. Ideals were something the sergeant-major couldn't begin to understand. There were simple bounds to his life and to his way of thought. Law and order were not dirty words to the CSM and he was proud of the fact. He did as he was told and he knew that his lords and masters knew better than he did about the decisions taken. What he enjoyed about soldiering was that those big decisions had been taken away from him and he only had to make the small adjustments that meant he stayed alive. He'd seen action in Malaya and Aden, he'd been in Cyprus and Belize, he'd trained in Germany and Norway, Australia and Canada, and he reckoned he'd seen the best days of the army, the days when 'Join the Army and See the World' had been true. Now the slogans were different and the attitudes had changed. For a soldier like Gilby it was all a matter of survival and doing things fast and efficiently.

He hadn't always been like that. Once he'd thought about the situations he was in. Read the papers, listened to informed opinion and he'd tried to make real judgements about the situations. That had stopped after Aden.

In Malaya he'd liked the people, all the people, and when he was on a jungle patrol against the terrorists, he had wondered if they weren't right in some ways. He'd done his job nevertheless and it hadn't worried him over much that people got killed in the process. That, after all, was what he was paid to do. In Cyprus the fighting had been uglier and the people more aggressive. He had never felt easy walking down Ledra Street, or along the peeling sea front in Larnaca. You never quite knew which of the bastards was carrying a gun or when you'd get one in the back. He smiled grimly. He didn't subscribe to the idiots in the press who talked about the cowards who fought there. No one in their right mind went up against a British soldier from the front. And he would be the first to admit that when those Greek Cypriots took to the hills, it was very hard to touch them. Their ground, their territory and they'd won something for themselves. But Aden was different.

There was nothing to like there and no one to admire. It was a shit-heap of a town and a treacherous, double-dealing evil little war. It was there he decided to stop worrying about the other side and to think only about himself and his side.

It wasn't anything to do with the piece of shrapnel still buried in his thigh but it was to do with the event that put it there.

They'd been on a patrol in three Land Rovers through the evil-smelling close-packed houses and the sun was high. The heat beat off the walls of the houses and shimmered off the piles of refuse on street corners. The dogs were lying panting in whatever shade they could find. No one had been on the street except the patrol.

His best mate was sitting beside him in the back of the Land Rover when three grenades rolled along the street and under the front Land Rover. As soon as they heard the dull, metallic clunk as the grenades hit the ground the second Land Rover carrying Gilby and his mate turned hard left and was instantly hit by small-arms fire. The driver got it in the face and Gilby and his mate dived off the back, rolling as they hit the ground and finishing up on opposite sides of the street against the mud walls of houses. Gilby opened up a burst and his mate yelled to him to get out while he covered him. Gilby ran for the street corner and turned it in time to see the first Land Rover blazing and shattered and the remnants of the patrol regrouping around the second Land Rover. For ten minutes they were all pinned down and then, as suddenly as it began, it was over. There was absolute silence in the streets. Gilby and the officer in charge moved gingerly around the street corner to look for Gilby's friend. He was there all right, and they'd been at him with a knife. Gilby

130

even now, sitting in the cool Irish morning, could suddenly feel his stomach heave. He had been sick on the spot when he saw what they'd done to his mate and from that moment he hadn't given a damn for anyone. Survive, and to hell with the rest. It was the same here, he thought.

Bilinski drove down the track with Two and Three Sections of Six Platoon in the Land Rovers and stopped where the track entered the quarry. He walked quickly across to Major Taylor, gave his report.

'She's cool, sir,' he said. 'Not a dicky-bird out of her.'

Major Taylor nodded.

'No sign of anyone there?' he asked and Bilinski shook his head.

'Nothing, sir. We didn't want to stir up too much. You didn't want her pushed too hard, sir,' he reminded the major.

'Just enough to make her make a move. Something to encourage her to panic, Sergeant,' said Major Taylor.

'Though from what you say she may not be the panicking sort. Where's Colour?'

'Back on the OP, sir. He'll report in if she moves.'

Major Taylor nodded and walked away to his Land Rover. He didn't want it to be a dead end but it looked very much as if it might be. He couldn't understand why Frank had taken to bombing small targets when his usual methods involved the big explosion and the grand gesture. It wasn't the pattern they'd come to expect and Major Taylor was beginning to wonder if Twiss had made a mistake.

'Twiss,' he said, and the soldier got quickly out of the back of the Land Rover and followed as his company commander walked slowly away from the other men in the platoon. Bilinski watched them both and knew that Taylor was having doubts about the whole thing. He looked across at Gilby, who grimaced and stayed put in his Land Rover.

'I'm certain, sir,' said Twiss. 'I know his face. I've

seen enough pictures. It was him.' Major Taylor nodded and walked on a little, then turned back to the soldier who, he could see, was angered by the doubts he had.

'It's all right, Twiss. Just don't want us all on a wild-goose chase, that's all. Carry on.'

Twiss turned and walked quickly back to the section. 'Bastard doesn't believe me,' thought Twiss. 'Five minutes with that woman and I'd've known for sure. Just five minutes.'

'Chewing them off, was he?' grinned Hunt, and Tompkins began to laugh.

'Shut your bloody mouth,' gritted Twiss to the young soldier and climbed back into the Land Rover.

The woman was still standing in the bedroom. She hadn't made any effort to clear up the mess left by the search. She stared at her reflection in the dressing-table mirror and watched the tears running down her face in an almost detached way. Suddenly she swept the bottles and brushes and lacy mats off the dressing-table onto the floor, where they smashed. She walked out of the room, leaving behind her the sickly-sweet smell of perfume and face cream congealing over the pile of clothes that had been left behind by the soldiers.

She was shaking with anger and fright. They had no right to walk into anyone's house and demand things. They had no right to trample through your home and open drawers and cupboards. They had no right to stand and stare and point their guns at you as if you were a pig for the slaughter.

She walked slowly down the stairs and into the front room. At the window she stopped and looked out. They were not there any more. She stared across at the broken-down yard and the mud and fallen stone walls and she hated the place. The years of looking after her mother, of trying to make up to her father for the fact that he had no son to take on the place, had made her bitter. Yet when Frank had first come into the house she had felt a warmth in the place and a feeling of care and love. He was a strong man and single-minded. He knew that she was lonely and he knew also that her mother gave her no peace and even less love. When they'd been together, times had been good and he'd even begun to mend the fence and to try to make the farm work again. She could've told him then that it wouldn't work but he'd seemed so happy and when he was away on his other work she'd only been afraid that he wouldn't come back.

When he was picked up by the British and put away in Long Kesh she hadn't heard for a week and she had had to suffer the anguish of not knowing what had happened without anyone to turn to. Her mother didn't care because she was already dying and Marie had no one else she could talk to about him.

He had liked the farm for its isolation, which suited his purpose ideally. She had always kept her promise never to tell anyone that he came there and her mother had died before she could tell anyone.

When he came out of Long Kesh he hadn't made any contact for months. He'd been away, he said, doing some training. Whatever had happened to him in that time in internment had hardened and embittered him. He admitted to her that he had been put away for good reason and he accepted it as a reasonable price to pay. But so many who were in the prison were innocent people who just happened to fit the book. They were pulled in for obscure reasons and without proof or charge against them. While it had embittered them it had made Frank a different man. Now he was certain and set in his part in the struggle. He was determined that he would never again go back into a camp and he was determined also that the injustices in the community would be avenged if they were not to be changed.

133

She knew that the organization was wary of Frank and that it had become more wary as time went by. He'd always done things his way because he didn't take orders from anyone, man or woman. 'Pussyfooting bastards,' he'd say at times when she asked him about the leadership. 'Hit them where it hurts.' But when he came out of the prison he hadn't come back to her.

She looked about the room and the sun glinted through the curtains and onto his old armchair. She told herself that he did care about her. That he stayed away because he was afraid she'd be compromised by him in the eyes of the Security Forces. She told herself the same thing every day that she didn't see him and every night when she went to her bed.

When he told her to drive a car to a pub or to arm a bomb in a van under a bridge she did it, even though she knew this wasn't his style and felt he was leading up to something much bigger. Hadn't he brought an old van into the yard one night with two large boxes marked for a blasting firm at the other side of the border? Hadn't she hidden that for him for a week and one day gone to the shed and found it had disappeared in the night? He hadn't even knocked at the door and passed the time of evening with her. She told herself Frank had his reasons and that when it was all over things would be fine between them again.

As for finding him to warn him she'd had a search, she didn't know where to begin looking and she knew that this was a danger. No doubt they'd still be looking and watching her from somewhere close by. She wasn't entirely a fool and she knew that a search like that was for something bigger. They knew that she knew Frank, so someone had been blabbing away in their place in the town or back in Belfast or somewhere. She sat down and stared at the empty grate and waited. She had one more thing to do.

134

Under the pines the observation post still waited and watched. They'd been there over eight hours and the strain of waiting had become a numb ache. No one moved unless he had to, no one took his eyes off the house or the road or the track down through the forest while he was on watch.

Adams glanced at his watch. 18:00 hours and the light behind them and they'd be in the dark, cold shadow of the pine trees. He shivered.

The woman down there in the house hadn't moved since they'd left. She seemed to Adams to be a drab woman. Somehow only when she was angry was she alive. She had fixed a smile on her face and used it as a defence. Nothing seemed to touch her except mention of Frank. She knew him all right, and she probably knew where he could be found, but she hadn't made a move yet.

Terry Adams had been puzzled by her. She'd made tea for them, had not made any resistance to the idea of her house being searched. She'd been afraid of them but he'd expected her to be angrier, louder in her condemnation of them. Other women would spit on soldiers as soon as look at them, women who were nothing but housewives and mothers. Not active women, in any case, but equipped with a deep and abiding suspicion of the army. Yet this woman hadn't done anything like that. It was almost as if the spirit had been knocked out of her and she had no further will to resist or even to express distaste at the idea of soldiers in her house.

He tried to imagine if any of the women he knew or had known would work with a man like Frank. It wasn't easy. 'Bugger her,' he muttered to himself, and stared back down at the house. It was in darkness. He looked again at his watch. She always switched on the light in the front room at 18:15. It was 18:15 now and there was no light. What was the woman doing?

Captain Simmons and Colour-Sergeant Jackson sat on

135

the damp earth beyond the first line of pines and talked quietly. 'She's very cool,' said Jacko. He leaned back against the bole of the tree and smelt the rich pine smell. He shut his eyes a moment and put his head back against the rough bark. Adams was right, he thought, we're bloody mad.

She wasn't going to crack, not now. It was too late. If she'd been going to move out she'd've done it by now. She'd had too much time to think about it and to put down the panic he'd seen in her eyes when they first confronted her on the step of her house.

He hated those searches, not because of the pain it caused was going fast now. Soon the sun would be the women, nor because he was afraid of what he might find. It was more fundamental than that for Jacko. He could see his wife in every woman's face and he knew what she would feel. He was getting soft, he thought, and opened his eyes. Captain Simmons was watching him.

'Tired?' he asked quietly and the colour-sergeant shook his head.

'No, sir. Just thinking about something one of the lads said to me.' The young captain waited. He admired this soldier and he knew that the colour-sergeant had a lot to offer, not only through his experience but also as a man. He was someone you had to respect for his professionalism and because he could think for himself and did.

'It's bloody funny, was what he said, sir,' said the colour-sergeant. 'And he's right. Us here watching her down there. She was quite a looker once,' said Jacko. The captain smiled.

'She's not that old now, Colour,' he said and Jacko shook his head.

'She looks worn out. Buggered,' he said.

'Her fault,' snapped the young captain and Jacko glanced across at him in surprise.

'She's involved. Right? She's carrying. She's carrying

136

the can back. She knows that. We catch her, she gets her lot. You know that, I do and so does she. If she wanted to look like Sleeping Beauty she'd've done well to stay out of it.' Captain Simmons leaned forward towards the colour-sergeant. 'You going soft on her?' he asked.

'No,' said Jacko mildly. 'Not soft. Pity though. An attractive woman, used up like that. Pity, that's all.'

The two men sat silently for a few moments. The sun had gone now and the cold shadow of early evening crept across the trees towards them.

'She won't move. You're right. We'll get 5 Platoon to take on this OP. I'll have a word with Lieutenant Preece. Simmons stood up on making the decision. Jackson stood up with him and nodded thoughtfully.

'OK, sir. Will I call into base or will you, sir?' 'You do it. I'll see you later.' Captain Simmons moved away quietly through the trees. As he did so Jacko heard the engine of a Gazelle spotter as it swooped for a last pass over the valley and the farm.

'Wasting your bloody time,' muttered Jacko to himself. 'Nothing's going to happen this time. A stand-up. False bloody alarm.' He turned up the track to give the men their orders.

The dark shadow fell across the valley and the house remained in darkness. Adams lay wondering what the woman was doing in the shabby, darkening rooms of her home over the hill.

Chapter Eight

Sergeant-Major Gilby had spent two weeks on leave and hated it. Two weeks of inactivity, just making time until he got back to barracks and the life he knew. He sat in his usual corner of the bar and watched as the barmaid pulled pints for the noisy mob in the other bar.

He supped up his pint, put down the glass and looked around the snug bar. There were a couple of long-haired kids in the corner with their girls and two more young men playing the fruit machine by the old fireplace. Gilby shook his head. What did they know about anything? Spending their lives in a round between office or factory and the boozer. Life was a thin feast for them, Gilby thought. No one talked to him.

He'd told the barmaid that he was expecting a little party tonight. His last night on leave and a few mates would be coming across from the Bedfords' barracks for a final drink up. They hadn't come because he hadn't seen anyone he knew in the local barracks.

'Same again, Mr Gilby?' The barmaid took up the glass and filled it before he could say anything. She put it onto the counter and he pulled out a note.

'Have one yourself, love,' he said.

'No, thanks. I've got one in, thanks,' she said. 'Didn't your friends turn up, then?'

'No. No, well, it was a casual arrangement. Not to worry.'

'And back tomorrow. Pity. We'll miss you. You're a bit of a fixture,' she said as she put his change down on the bar mat.

She was an attractive woman in an overblown sort of way.

'Listen,' he said. 'What time d'you finish tonight?'

She smiled. 'About eleven. Why?'

'Thought you might fancy a bite to eat. That's all.' She looked at him, still smiling, and shook her head.

'I might like it, Mr Gilby. I'm not sure my husband would. He picks me up every Sunday about then. Sorry.'

Gilby picked up his drink and found that someone had taken his chair by the bar. He walked across to the table where the two lads were chatting up their girls.

'Anyone's chair?' he asked, gesturing to the spare one by the table.

'Help yourself, mate,' said one of the boys and the two girls began to laugh. He sat down and smiled at the boys.

'Come in a lot, do you?' he asked by way of conversation.

'Weekends,' said the pale, black-haired boy with no beef on him. Gilby drank up and looked at the boy across the top of his glass.

'We don't see you that often, do we?' said the other lad. 'No,' said Gilby. 'You wouldn't. I'm a soldier. On leave, see?'

One of the girls whispered to her friend and the two of them got up and walked away from the table.

'What about you?' asked Gilby.

'Down the bank,' said the second youth. 'Clerks.'

Gilby smiled patronizingly and put down his glass. 'You surprise me, you do. So many of you lads stuck in offices - no outdoors, no action. Just counting money and filling ledgers. Funny sort of life for a young lad.' The two young men sat back and said nothing.

'Look,' said the sergeant-major, 'you've got no exciting things to look forward to, have you? Not like us. Still, it takes all sorts.'

'What, for example?' asked one of the lads. 'What've you got, mister, that's so great? A soldier!' He grinned and drank up.

139

'It's a job worth doing. Now I wouldn't press the Queen's Shilling on any man. But I tell you, it's a good life. Ordered, disciplined, and exciting at times. Oh yes. I could tell you a tale or two . . .' Sergeant-Major Gilby wanted to talk about Cyprus or Aden but the two girls came back and told the young men it was time they went home.

'How about a drink first?' suggested Gilby.

'No, thanks,' said the first young man. 'Another time maybe. Tarrah.' And the four youngsters walked out of the snug.

Tom Gilby looked at his beer. It suddenly tasted sour and he didn't want to waste any more time sitting in that place. He wanted desperately to be back again on the square, knowing where he stood. Jacko and Bilinski, Captain Simmons and Major Taylor . . . they'd feel the same, he knew that for sure. No soldier felt easy outside. No one wanted you and yet they were glad enough to have you when the shit hit the fan, Gilby thought bitterly. He looked across at the bar clock. It was nearly closing time and he'd be able to sleep soon.

The large clock in the corner of the room ticked away steadily. Jacko walked in after his mother-in-law and helped her off with her coat. They'd had a good meal out as a goodbye gesture from the in-laws and he'd avoided having to meet their ex-army friends at the club. He'd been glad about that. He didn't fancy talking to that ex-major who kept his title and drank himself red-eyed every night and talked about his bloody war all the time.

He'd talked quietly when he had to and didn't drink too much and he knew that Mary was pleased it'd gone off so well. She'd been worried that he'd get steamed up and say too much.

'Nice evening,' he said, as he put the coat on a chair.

'They do a good meal,' said his mother-in-law. 'You

140

were very quiet, Jack. Thinking about work tomorrow, I suppose.'

He was surprised that she should mention it. She hadn't said anything when he'd told them about his promotion. He hadn't felt that they were pleased or excited for him and he'd resented that. Perhaps they didn't understand what it meant to a gash private to command a platoon. They understood the officers and didn't have a clue about the men. It wasn't their fault, perhaps, but it niggled him.

'Jack.' Mrs Barker looked worried. 'Will you be going back . . . you know . . . to Ireland? Soon?' she asked. He shook his head. 'I don't know,' he said. 'Mary won't be. We've done our garrison tour for a bit, so don't worry about her.'

Mrs Barker found it difficult to talk to him, he knew that. He didn't understand why and she'd never tried to explain it.

'I do worry. We both do, Jack. Not just for Mary.' It was the nearest she'd ever come to saying that she cared for him. He was surprised by it and looked at his watch because he didn't know what to say to this elderly, prim and worried woman.

'They're taking a time locking up,' he said.

Mrs Barker walked away from him and wound up the clock. 'He enjoys it when you come down,' she said without turning to him. 'He feels stimulated, he says.'

Jacko shook his head disbelievingly. 'I think it's because he enjoys the kids and Mary. I've always thought that. I've always thought I annoyed him. Both of you, to tell the truth.' She turned back to him, and he saw the hurt in her eyes. 'I know what you expected. Something better than a gash private. You would expect that. I know that,' he said. He hated saying it and he didn't want this woman to feel hurt by him.

She sighed. 'Jack, you frightened us. That's the truth.

141

You still do. You are hard, ambitious. It's something we're not used to. My husband has never been aggressive or hard. It's not something we're used to,' she repeated lamely.

'I suppose not. Maybe he hasn't had to be,' said Jacko bitterly. 'D'you mind if I have a drink?'

He knew that whenever they saw each other she retreated. She refused to enter into discussions because she was afraid that they were in fact arguments, and she couldn't stand the tension and the anger that simmered beneath the surface when he began to talk seriously about anything. He put the stopper back into the decanter and turned to her.

'It's funny, really. Coming back here is like nothing on earth.' He smiled. 'You take a long time winding down after a garrison tour. You get tense, edgy with your family even. It's not easy to live with, I don't suppose.' He walked across the room towards the elderly lady. 'Maybe they should lock us away for a month to cool off. I don't know. Still, I'm glad we came here. So're the kids. They like it. At least it's normal.'

Jack took a drink and she moved towards him. He couldn't remember the last time she had even touched his arm and tonight she did for a moment, tried to say something but found it impossible. 'Jack . . . I . . . Jack.

The door opened and Mary and her dad came in and the moment had gone. Mrs Barker had never really begun to understand the tension and maybe it wasn't fair to try and make her. She had a nice home, she liked her grandchildren and loved Mary, and he, well, he was part of it now, whether she liked it or not, and that was that.

The two women left the men to have their nightcap. 'Don't be long, Jacko,' smiled Mary, and walked out with her mother. The two men settled by the fire with the decanter between them and talked in a desultory way for a time.

'It's not easy, you know. For her. Mrs Barker,' the older man said quietly. 'She was worried sick all the time you were away. And she missed the kids.' He poured himself a small measure and pushed the decanter across to Jacko.

'I am sorry about that lad who got killed. Very sorry.'

'Yes,' said Jacko. 'You said. Now forget it. Please.' He raised his glass to the older man and they both drank. The clock ticked steadily. Jacko leaned back in his chair and sighed. He was warm, had a drink in his hand and was reasonably happy, and tomorrow the work would begin again and he'd have to lick Six Platoon into some sort of shape. It wouldn't be easy, he knew that, and he knew too that he was going to do it and do it well.

'I remember once, in India . . . you know that Mrs Barker's family was out there? I was a raw subaltern,' said the older man, staring bleakly at the fire. 'Just joined. Just before the war, in fact. It was all romance and adventure then. Ride down against the Frontier . . . all Kipling and Empire.' He laughed nervously. To excuse his own enthusiasm for the time, thought Jacko. 'No one worried about the politicians, not really. The army was there, the King was on his throne and all was well in the world. It really was like that. I didn't have a bean to my name. I joined anyway and we led the life of Riley. Until one day I was posted up-country and spent four months on the Frontier.'

He glanced across at Jacko and the soldier knew that the old man was trying hard to tell him something about himself.

'It wasn't easy, it wasn't pleasant and it was very lonely.'

Jacko was surprised. All he'd ever heard before from the old man was how much he had enjoyed army life.

'I've never told anyone this, Jack.' The old man wouldn't look at him now, 'I hated it. I knew then I wasn't

143

made to be a soldier but then the war started and I was stuck. No way out. Then we went to Burma and that was ugly and real and very frightening. The tension. It makes or breaks you, I think.'

Jacko said nothing. Just looked across at the older man and waited for him to finish.

'I don't expect you to agree with me. You never do.' Mr Barker smiled softly and took a drink.

Jacko refilled the older man's glass and then his own. 'Your wife just told me I frighten you, well, her anyway,' he said. Mr Barker waited. 'Mary and I are OK, you know. We get on fine.' The old man said nothing still. 'I just thought you should know, sir. That's all.'

The old man nodded for a moment and then stood up. Time for my shut-eye, I think, Jack. Goodnight. Put out the light when you come up.' He walked out of the room and closed the door quietly. Jacko sat down again and stared at the flames, and quite suddenly he could smell burning flesh. Poor bloody soldier, he thought. Poor bastard. Ended before it began for him and all Tom Gilby could say was 'Silly bastard. He could've blown the lot. Playing heroes.' What a bastard way to go. In bits, in a wet, windy, soft evening in a small town in Ireland. Jacko drank the dregs, leaned back in the chair and began to sleep.

Already the dark shadows had fallen across the hillside and the silence amongst the trees was even deeper than usual. The sky was a pale yellow through the low grey cloud and though it wasn't yet raining the air was heavy and damp with the coming storm. Adams wriggled backwards from his observation position and joined the rest of the recce section on the track down to the Land Rover. He was as glad as the rest to be off the post.

Captain Simmons had sent in a relief section and told Colour to get his men back to the location in town. It'd be a decent night's kip, Adams thought. That's something, at

144

least.

'All here?' asked Jacko, and checked them off as they climbed into the back of their Land Rover. No one spoke as they drove down the track and turned out onto the road. No one asked Adams what the search had turned up, no one wanted to speak. They were too tired to be bothered and they'd all be too tired to eat when they got back to the town location. Adams glanced across at Mayhoe, who was leaning on his loaded rifle and staring at the floor of the Land Rover.

'What are you doing this leave then, Johnny?' Adams said eventually. The black soldier looked up at him and shook his head.

'I'm sleeping, man, and then I'm going to dance with my bird and drink a bit and then sleep some more. Believe me.'

Adams looked out of the back of the Land Rover into the slight light of the evening. The countryside looked so peaceful during the day and it was only at night, driving through these narrow lanes and past the ivy-covered walls, that there was any feeling of menace in the air. The soldier shivered and shoved his hands inside his jacket for warmth.

'You?' asked Johnny Mayhoe.

Adams shrugged. 'I dunno,' he said. 'See the wife . . . that's all, really. I dunno.'

The other soldiers lolled against the thudding and bucking of the Land Rover. Some of them were dull-eyed for lack of sleep. The soldier at the back nursed his SLR and pointed it vaguely out of the back of the vehicle and the rest sat vacantly almost, swaying with the motion as the Land Rover drove them through enemy country back to base.

The woman stirred herself from the armchair and glanced at the clock. She hadn't moved from the chair

145

since the soldiers had left her alone. The room was shadowed as the sun dipped down. She looked around the room blearily, as if she'd just woken. She hadn't slept, but a sort of lethargy had overtaken her and she recognized that it was something to do with reaction to the searching and the soldiers. She had never had to face the soldiers before and she felt sick at the memory.

On the table the bits of paper that bore the phone number the young soldier had given her lay like so much confetti.

She'd have to warn Frank, of course, but she had no idea how she would do it. She didn't know where he had stayed since he had come out of prison. She'd asked him often enough and he'd always been angry when she did.

'What you don't know you can't tell them,' he said, and that was an end of it. She looked at the clock. Twenty minutes to wait before she did as she had been ordered.

They'd sat in a lay-by on the other side of town and Frank had laughed when he told her what to do.

'They'll expect the same again,' he'd said. 'Something small, something useless. They'll already have had two little ones and they'll be expecting the same again.'

He'd leaned back in the passenger seat and laughed. She hadn't dared to ask him what was going to happen. She knew better than that.

The woman stirred herself and got up. She walked slowly upstairs and into her bedroom and looked again at the mess. The smell of the spilt perfume reeked through the room. Without his things strewn about the room it seemed very empty. She closed the door and walked back through the dark house, past the room that had been her mother's and back down the stairs into the hall where the telephone stood. The woman was afraid now, afraid not only of the soldiers but also of Frank.

Sometimes, when they'd met briefly, he'd been shaking with anger at the idea of soldiers in the Province.

She'd tried to make him talk about things but he refused. She knew that the other active service units in the area were afraid of him. He wouldn't toe the line and work with anyone. His fight seemed to be a personal matter and if that endangered others he didn't appear to be worried about that.

The woman stopped at the bottom of the stairs as a thought struck her. She wondered if he cared about her. Just for a moment the thought nagged her and she hurriedly shut it out but it was already eating away like a canker in her mind.

She'd done as she was told because, at first, it was an adventure and because Frank had insisted that he was right. But he had become more reckless and his targets had become more and more of a risk. Not to him, for he was rarely on the scene when they went up. The risk was for other people, innocent people who were not part of the fight. Sometimes this worried the woman, but she had never talked with Frank about it. He wouldn't have discussed it anyway.

The woman walked along the hall to the phone.

The Land Rover stopped at Sergeant Bilinski's road block. 'We're going in now, Pete,' said Jacko from the passenger seat.

'Lucky you,' said the sergeant. He was cold and his men were fed up with the routine of setting up vehicle check points only to be told to move on and set up another elsewhere. These random checks rarely revealed anything, but the pattern of harassment meant that people in the area never quite knew where the army would appear next. It also meant that the innocent were annoyed by the constant demands for information which was noted down by the man in charge of each VCP.

'Where have you come from, sir? Licence please, sir. May we search your car, sir? Where are you proceeding, sir?' Everyone was heartily sick of the polite fictions. A man in a car stopped by six armed soldiers was hardly likely to refuse to allow them to search or have his papers. They'd get out of the car, open the boot and wait, weary and bored, for the search to be done and for the man in charge to hand back the papers.

'Thank you very much, sir. Have a good journey. Thank you, sir.'

And the men on the check point would stand watching as the man drove away on his own business and they'd be left in the damp of the night on a lonely road with little shelter. Bilinski watched as the tail lights of the Land Rover headed into the murky evening. It was still light enough to see down over the valley and along its flat bottom as far as the lake.

'Sick of it,' said Twiss. 'Sick and bloody fed up of it.' Bilinski turned to give him a mouthful just as the radio squawked in the leading Land Rover. He walked quickly across to it.

'Two three. Send. Over.'

In the command room a young lieutenant sat on the table and watched the signaller talking into his radio. He'd come down from Stranmoore an hour ago and it'd been a routine night. Some men were asleep in their bunks at the top of the old police station; others were working on the wrecked Pig that had been brought back for safety to the location; the men in the sangars over the gates were checking people in and out.

In the cookhouse the white-aproned cooks were working flat out for the section that had just come in and were also preparing for the OP party when it appeared in base.

A few soldiers were in the recreation room, thumbing through old numbers of girly papers or trying to find the last few pages of the ancient and tattered westerns and war books in the makeshift bookshelves by the telly.

A few nights of quiet routine, the young officer thought, would do us very nicely. We'll go out 'not with a bang but a whimper', and be damned glad of it. He grinned to himself and slid off the table as Company Sergeant-Major Gilby walked into the Ops room.

'Evening, sir,' said the older man and the lieutenant nodded a tight smile at him. He had never been sure how to react to Tom Gilby, though he knew that Major Taylor regarded him very highly.

'Evening, Sergeant-Major. Quiet on all fronts?' he asked. Gilby grunted and checked the message pad by the signaller. It was blank.

'Major Taylor been in, sir?' asked the sergeant-major. The officer shook his head.

'He's coming in later.'

It was all too quiet for Tom Gilby. He, like Major Taylor, expected something to break very soon and, again like the major, he was not sure that the two small bombs they'd had in the area were the work of Frank.

He felt certain they were placed by small operators and that Frank had moved out of the area as soon as he'd known he'd been spotted. If that snatch squad had moved faster, if the people in Belfast hadn't pussyfooted around . . . if, if, if.

The phone began to ring at the other end of the control room. The signaller picked it up and listened for a moment before handing the phone to the lieutenant.

He listened, then gestured for the pad, which the signaller passed to him. He began to write.

'Yes,' he said. 'Hang on a moment, please. Your name, madam. Your name, please?' He slowly put the phone down and pushed the message across to Sergeant-Major Gilby.

'CAR OUTSIDE ANDREWS PAINT STORES'. That was all it said.

'She rang off,' he said.

'She?' asked Gilby.

'No name. The usual. Just that message and she rang off.' Gilby had already located the paint stores at the far side of town.

'Here, sir.' He pointed.

'Contact Major Taylor. Tell him,' said the lieutenant. 'Tell him I'll take a patrol down. We'll need more men, Sergeant-Major.'

'Call in Sergeant Bilinski's road block. He's near enough. And Jacko's on his way in from the OP. Call him up too, sir? Divert them. Usual drill, sir?' asked the sergeant-major.

'Usual drill,' confirmed the lieutenant and walked quickly out of the Ops room.

Gilby was beginning to enjoy himself.

'Call up Colour,' he said to the signaller. 'I'll get Felix out.' He picked up the phone and began dialling the bomb disposal unit. As he waited for the call to be connected he called across to the signaller. 'And divert Sergeant Bilinski. We'll need a platoon strength down there. House-to-house and the lot. Clear the area. Tell him. OK? I'll RV down there with them.'

The lieutenant came back in. 'Ready, Sergeant-Major?' he asked. 'Stand-by section is ready to go now. Major Taylor?' 'Just raised him, sir,' said the signaller. 'He's going direct. RV with you there, sir.'

Gilby turned to the corporal who came into the Ops room to report his section was ready.

'Get the rest of Six Platoon out, Corporal. I want the area saturated. Clear?'

The corporal nodded and went out fast. Outside they could hear the engines beginning to turn over and the clatter of armed men mounting the Land Rovers and Pigs.

Upstairs the men were turning out, struggling to find their boots and rifles, and racing down the stairs in the dark.

150

By the time Sergeant-Major Gilby had finished talking to Felix and leaving messages for the signaller Six Platoon was already on its way out of the iron gates.

The street of terraced houses was quiet as Jacko and recce section drove past. At the main gates to the paint factory the Land Rover stopped and Jacko stepped up to the locked double doors and rattled them.

'Come on,' he yelled. 'Open up! Open up!'

He looked back at the section as they fanned out of the Land Rover. They were taking care where they trod and making sure they stayed in the shadow of the factory wall. Too many times a patrol had been called out, only to find that they had walked into an ambush.

Jacko was pleased at the way the men melted into the dark shadows but he felt very exposed himself, though he knew that Adams would have had him well covered from the other side of the road.

He banged the gates again, and as he did so the two Land Rovers of Bilinski's patrol squealed around the corner and slammed to a stop. Before they'd cut their engines the men of Two and Three Sections had got out and deployed up the street in both directions, to prevent anyone coming down either way and also to make sure that no one left the houses at the far end.

Jacko looked along the road and could only see three cars left in the parking area near the terrace of houses. Sergeant Bilinski joined him at the run.

'Bloody night-watchman's taking his time,' said Jacko, and as he did so the small Judas gate opened and an elderly man poked his head out.

'What is it you're wanting?' he asked angrily.

Already people were beginning to peer out of their houses along the road. Some were standing on the doorsteps watching the soldiers; others were already wandering down to the nearest Land Rover to find out what was going on. A few of the young men began to shout at the soldiers and to make throat-cutting gestures with their fingers.

Jacko glanced across the dreary street and called, 'Adams!' Adams doubled across the road to the factory gates.

'Colour?'

'Keep them at that end of the street. I don't want any of them down here. Get on with it.'

Adams nodded and turned. He ran across to Twiss and Mayhoe and the three of them walked purposefully up the street towards the gathering crowd. Their rifles held casually in the crook of their arms, they walked steadily to the front of the crowd and the people moved back slowly. Jacko watched as Tompkins joined the three shepherding the women and kids back along the street.

'What is it you want?' asked the watchman again.

'There's a car here that shouldn't be here,' said Jacko. 'You know them, so you show us. All right?' said Jacko. The man hesitated. He didn't want to get involved.

'A bloody bomb, is it?' asked the man.

'I don't know yet,' said Jacko. 'Now take a look for us.'

The man stepped reluctantly between the sergeant and the colour-sergeant and walked cautiously along the road beside the factory wall. It wasn't until they came close to the blue Ford Cortina that the man stopped.

'That one,' he said. 'Not one of ours.' He refused to go any closer.

Jackson nodded. 'OK,' he said. 'You'd better stay out of it. Leave the door open and get up the road.'

The watchman didn't wait to argue. He turned and walked quickly away, leaving the two soldiers staring at the car.

'Check it with records, Bil,' said Jacko. 'And then I want your lads to check the area. All of it. And don't touch a thing, Bil. Right?'

Bilinski took a note of the number of the car and walked across to his Land Rover.

Colour-Sergeant Jackson joined Adams and the men from Six Platoon who were standing facing the locals. No one was talking and the soldiers stood with their rifles at the ready.

'What is it, then, Sergeant?' a woman yelled.

Jackson shrugged and turned to Tompkins. 'Steady, lad,' he said and Tompkins smiled nervously.

'Found it, Colour?' asked Adams quietly.

'Maybe. Could be a joker, couldn't it?'

Sergeant Bilinski's men were already carefully checking the other cars and the area around them to make sure that there were no suspicious parcels, unidentifiable objects and the like around the area. It was necessary work before the bomb disposal boys got in to sort the car out.

Jacko walked quickly across to Sergeant Bilinski. 'Well?' he asked.

'Stolen,' said the sergeant. 'It's another all right, I'd say.'

'Would you?' said Jackson acidly, and walked quickly across to the Land Rover that had just nosed through the crowd. Major Taylor got out.

'What're they doing here?' asked the major gesturing at the crowd. 'I want them off the street. And not in their houses, Colour-Sergeant. I want all the houses cleared.'

'Sir,' said Colour-Sergeant Jackson and snapped about and across to the section covering the crowd.

'Adams, Mayhoe, you, Twiss . . . Tompkins. Take one side of the street. In pairs. I want the houses emptied. Everyone in the area to be got out. Sergeant Bilinski!' he called. 'A section of men to clear these people off the street. Block both ends and no one comes down. All right?'

'Yes, Colour.'

'What's going on, soldier?' yelled a woman. 'Made a fuck up again, have you?' The crowd laughed as the

153

soldier turned to her fast.

'I want you off the street, lady, and out of those houses. I want no one left behind. Clear? That's a bomb we have down there and you're likely to get it just like us if you don't clear off the street.'

They didn't believe him. They'd heard it so many times before in various parts of the Province and they were apathetic and disinterested. 'You heard me,' repeated Jackson. 'Off the street, right off. Now move it.' He watched as a few people began to disperse from the back of the crowd, and slowly the people turned away up the street.

Felix, the bomb disposal unit captain, turned through the crowd and down towards the knot of soldiers.

Bilinski and Jackson walked with Major Taylor to his Land Rover.

'Frank again, Sir?' asked Bilinski.

'Don't know,' answered the major and gave the signaller instructions about checking on the fire brigade, the RUC, the local hospital and HQ. While he was doing that the bomb disposal captain walked quickly up the street, ignoring the other soldiers and the crowd.

'Which one?' he asked and Jackson pointed out the Cortina. Felix nodded and went back to his Land Rover to begin getting together his equipment. Jackson went with him.

The area been cleared?' asked the captain.

'Doing it now, sir,' said Jackson. 'It could be Frank's work again.'

'Hell,' said the captain and grinned. 'Pity about the car. It looks new-ish.'

'You'll burn it, will you?' asked the colour-sergeant and Felix nodded. 'If it's in the car and it is Frank's work I'm not going to mess about opening doors, I can tell you. We'll have a nice controlled bang and that'll be that. You clearing the houses?'

Twiss and Mayhoe had cleared their side of the street, for now with the bomb disposal unit in the street, the crowd realized it was serious and no one was anxious to stay and get themselves blown to bits. Apart from some anxious mothers and kids, they had no trouble clearing the houses out. Tompkins and Adams were having a more difficult time. An old woman was stubbornly refusing to get out.

'Not for you, son. Not for anyone. This is my home. I'm not coming out.' The old woman stood on her step facing the two young soldiers. She was over sixty and looked frail enough for a puff of wind to blow over. But she refused to budge.

'You've got to come out, lady,' said Adams. 'It'll blow as likely as not, and then where'll you be? Eh?'

'Come on out, love,' said Tompkins. 'You can't stay in there. You're too close to the car. Now come out and use your loaf, please.'

The old woman shook her head and began to shut her door. Adams shoved his foot against it and she hesitated a moment and then walked away down the hall into the house.

'What's going on, Adams?' yelled Jacko. 'Clear them all, I said.'

'She won't move, Colour,' said Adams.

'So, let her stew. Leave her for the RUC. Their problem. I want the area round the car checked and cleared for Felix. Come on, you've got work.' Adams nodded and walked quickly across to Twiss and Mayhoe, who were already walking back to join the rest of the platoon near the cars. Tompkins didn't move.

'You heard me, Tompkins. Move it,' said Jackson.

'But, Colour,' he said, 'she's an old woman. What happens if that bloody car goes up?'

'Her problem,' said Jackson and walked away. Tompkins hesitated a moment and then followed him.

155

'But, Colour, she said it's her home. She's old. She doesn't understand.'

Jackson turned on the soldier savagely. 'She knows all right. She knows like anyone else here. Now do as you're told, soldier.'

Jackson joined Tom Gilby, who had just arrived.

'All clear, Colour?' asked the sergeant-major.

'Except for an old bird. The police can do her, sir. It'll be a small one anyway. If it's like the others.'

'*If* it is?' asked Gilby.

'Same pattern. Aimless really, isn't it?' said Jackson, as they watched the bomb disposal captain set up his 'wheelbarrow'.

'Wonders of modern science,' muttered Bilinski. He stood at their side and watched. The little machine looked like a tank and was able to relay pictures back to the bomb disposal team from the inside of the car. As it worked by remote control there was little danger to anyone at this stage.

The 'wheelbarrow' began to move slowly towards the car as the soldiers took up positions at a distance from the target.

The evening was darkening fast and Six Platoon had managed to rig up some extra lights in the street, focused on the car. The little tank moved erratically towards the target. Felix watched his small television screen carefully and guided the machine from his Land Rover.

Tompkins was worried. He leaned across to Adams, who was crouched in a doorway out of the line of any blast that might occur.

'What about that old bird?' he whispered, and Adams shrugged.

'Her problem. I told her to move. If it blows we all get it. She refused,' he went on. 'If I carry her kicking and screaming someone's gonna say I assaulted her. Her problem, mate. Now shurrup about her.'

Tompkins looked down the deserted end of the street. No one was keen now to be where the soldiers were. He felt thirsty and suddenly very scared. Everyone was watching the jerky progress of the 'wheelbarrow'. It stopped alongside the car and began to scan it.

Bilinski and Jacko leaned together in the angle of the factory wall. Jackson was chewing over the problem out loud.

'It's not right, a small bomb here. What the hell is the point of it?'

'No point in the one by the pub. All it did was blow a wall down. Nothing else,' muttered Bilinski.

Suddenly Jackson knew what it was about. A bomb outside a paint factory didn't make much sense, but one inside would.

'Jesus,' he breathed. 'Jesus wept. A trigger. He plants a little bomb outside . . . they let us know . . . and he's got a big one inside . . .' Jacko sprinted across to Felix's truck.

Major Taylor and the captain were watching the picture being relayed back from the Cortina.

'Sir,' Jacko called. 'Anything there, sir?' Felix adjusted the controls and smiled. 'Yes,' he said. 'Not very big. Something on the back seat. Look.'

Both men peered at the picture. There on the back seat of the car was a small parcel. Beside it, a clock connected to the parcel with a length of wire.

'Cheeky bastard. Doesn't even bother to hide it,' said the captain.

'What will you do?' asked Major Taylor and the captain glanced at him.

'Burn it,' he said. 'If it's Frank I'm not getting too close.'

'We don't know, do we?' said the major. I'd like proof, you see?'

'You're asking me to defuse it, are you?' asked the captain.

157

'You could tell then. Right?'

The captain nodded. 'Sure. If it's Frank's work I'll know all right. He has his own systems. I'd know OK.'

'Sir,' said Jackson. 'Just a thought, sir. If our lad has been planting little bombs about as a blind . . . if there's something bigger in there . . . in the stores. . . . See what I mean, sir?'

The captain looked round at the colour-sergeant. 'On a trembler?'

Jacko nodded. 'It'd be a trigger, sir, see? There's thousands of gallons of paint, thinners and God knows what in there. If this car goes up, if you made a mistake, sir, then that detonation will send up the lot. If all that paint goes up, sir, it could set half this town alight.'

'And me,' said Felix grinning. 'And bloody me.'

For a moment no one said anything. The captain stared at the flickering picture of the small bomb in the back of the car and then at Major Taylor.

'Colour,' said the major. 'Check it. Inside. Sergeant Bilinski, move those people from the far end of the street as far away as you can. I'll sort the police. Move it. Tell them if they don't bloody move they could find themselves lit up with burning paint and thinners. Right?'

Jackson was already half-way to the gates of the factory. Adams and Mayhoe were with him as he went through the judas gate.

Chapter Nine

Adams lay in bed and stared at the ceiling of the room he and Tsai had in his parents' house. She refused to stay with his mom and dad for much longer and he knew that he had to find a quarter as soon as he got back to Tidworth.

He looked across at Tsai as she lay asleep on the pillow beside him. Her long black hair gleamed in the early morning light and he wanted to tell her how sorry he was that nothing had gone right this leave. Whenever he wanted to make love with her he'd failed. The tension of that tour was still not drained out of him and his constant failure with Tsai had only made it worse.

Today he was due to report back to the battalion and he knew that if she asked him he'd be tempted not to go. He'd had enough of it all and could hardly see any point in what they were doing. 'Playing bloody soldiers on Salisbury Plain,' was how that man described it last night in the pub.

They'd been sitting very quietly together, hardly talking, and he came across, half drunk, and swayed to a stop by their table.

Mr Lyons was an old mate of his dad's and he'd known Terry Adams since he was a kid.

'Bloody hell,' he'd said. 'Bloody hell, back on leave again. I don't know what the taxpayers get out of you soldiers. Playing bloody soldiers on Salisbury Plain. Waste of taxpayers' money, you.'

Terry hadn't thought twice. He had reached for the bottle that stood on the table and was going to zap the drunk before he said any more and he had found the bottle had gone. He looked round and saw Tsai smiling up at him, the bottle lying in her lap.

'Terry,' she'd said. 'He's drunk. Not worth it.' The older man had eventually gone back to the bar. Suddenly

159

Terry had wanted to get out of that pub and away from them all. None of them gave a monkey's about him, not about any of them. They weren't even his kind any more. He hated coming home.

Terry lay back on the pillow and shut his eyes. Beside him Tsai stirred, then opened her eyes and looked at him. Their faces were close together and she kissed him gently.

'I'm sorry, Tsai,' he said softly, and she smiled at him. I'm sorry about last night.' She put a finger on his mouth and said nothing. 'I wanted to, I did want to. I couldn't. I just couldn't. I'm very sorry.' He didn't know how to explain to her.

'It'll be all right when we've got a quarter, Terry,' she said. 'Won't it?' Her large brown eyes watched him and he squirmed into a sitting position.

'It's that soldier, isn't it?' she asked quietly, and he nodded and shut his eyes. He couldn't get the sight of it out of his mind.

'It will go,' she said quietly.

He knew it'd go. You'd always be able to forget about this or that bloke, dead, knocked off. It was, after all, what you came to expect in the army. It wasn't as if you didn't care. You did, for a time. But if you remembered all the accidents and some of the deaths, you'd never do anything. By the time they had all got back on that square at Tidworth this afternoon no one would mention Tompkins. He'd be another statistic and only later would they begin to embroider stories around what happened to him. For the moment he would be dead and forgotten.

Tsai moved over the bed to him and kissed him again. He felt the soft touch of her long hair across his body and her cool, strong lips against his and he wanted her.

'Terry,' she whispered as he struggled away from her. He couldn't do anything. 'I'm sorry,' he said again, angry with himself. The memory of that afternoon outside the paint factory nagged away at the wrong moments. It was

160

like his mother when he was a kid. He would come in late and be creeping up the stairs to his bed and she'd call out, 'Terry? Terry, is that you?' As if it'd be anyone else in the place. She'd lie awake and trap him every time he came in. Nagging at him, denying his freedom, demanding affection without giving it, demanding obedience while at the same time destroying his father, demanding attention without ever listening. It was no wonder, he thought, that the first chance he'd got he'd signed on. Tsai lay quietly in his arms and made no more attempts at loving. He stroked a strand of hair from her forehead and she looked up at him.

'You haven't talked about it, Terry. You haven't told me about it. I want to help you. Tell me, please.'

Terry lay back on his arm and sighed. He shut his eyes a moment and tried not to think about it all.

'You wouldn't let me come with you. I wanted to come. You can tell me, surely, then I'll know. Next time I come with you,' said the Malay girl. And she touched the side of his face gently.

Terry began to talk slowly, groping for the right words, and soon he poured it out as though a dam had broken and all the anger and frustration of the past months were able to spew away with his talking.

'. . . patrols, women spitting on us, yes, and kids swearing at us. Men standing in doorways watching us go by and running their fingers across their throats when we look at them. That. All that. You go out on a foot patrol, you get the lot. No one'll talk to you in some places and in others they kiss your arse and give you cups of tea and d'you know, d'you know, I hate them just as much because they're part of it. Part of the reason, just as much as the others. They're just as much part of us losing that kid as the rest. Only a kid. They tell you you've got a trade. Sure I have. Killing. I'm good at that. Very good at it.'

Tsai rolled away and turned her back for a moment. He reached out and touched her and she turned to look at him.

161

She had never seen him like this, never heard the anger and bitterness in his voice before.

'You asked me to tell you. Well?' he asked.

'Go on, Terry. Please. Go on,' she said.

He drew a breath, leaned across to the chair by the bed and fumbled for cigarettes. He lit one before he began again more quietly.

'Little kids throwing stones, see. Draw you up streets to an ambush. Planned. Eight, nine years old and doing that. Little kids, yeah. Girls'd chat up the lads and they'd go off from a disco on the camp maybe to a party. It'd be a party with the wrong end of an Armalite or a Kalashnikov. That's happened. They think you do all that and laugh. I've thought about it, Tsai, this leave. I've thought about it.' He lay back and dragged smoke in from the cigarette. Tsai was quiet, waiting for him to go on.

The bloke last night. He was lucky he didn't lose his eyes. You know that. If he had, though, he'd not change. Not really. He'd not bloody change if I kicked the five colours of shit out of him either. I'd've proved his point in some way. It's what he expects. Thugs in uniform, that's us to him. Well, someone has to do it for the blokes upstairs. They'll not do their own dirty work, get gobbed on from the flats, shot at, stoned. I know why they do it and I sometimes think they're right. We've all been gobbed on from a great height. By them upstairs.' Terry lay with the cigarette dangling across the edge of the bed. Tsai moved towards him and took his hand. He didn't notice her.

'Give them one night patrol through the Creggan, or a day in a location in Armagh or half a day and a night in a stinking bog . . . They'd be chuffed to hell, wouldn't they?' They lay in silence for a long time. Terry finished his cigarette and stubbed it by the side of the bed. He looked across at Tsai and was surprised to see that she was crying. He didn't understand what had happened, what had made

162

her cry. He had never seen her in tears before.

'Tsai,' he said, touching her. 'Tsai, what's the matter?' She turned to him and pushed her arms around his neck and clung to him. She sobbed against his shoulder and he tried hard to comfort her, without success. 'Tsai, tell me what's the matter. Don't cry.'

'Don't go back,' she said, muffled against his flesh. 'Don't go back.'

'I have to go back. I have to go,' he said. 'What d'you mean?'

'They change you, Terry. They change you. You never were like this. You never came home like this before. You . . . you seem to be sick almost. I've never heard you angry before and you are now, aren't you? Very angry?'

Terry stared again at the ceiling as the girl clung to him. 'Yes, I suppose,' he said.

'Why? You have a job. You do the job. You know what the job is. You did the same in other places. Something like it. Now suddenly it is different. Why are you so angry?'

Adams, lying in Tsai's bedsitter in Swindon, could see the woman on the farm. Quite suddenly she was in his mind and he knew that the terror she had experienced, the fear they had brought her, the cold, casual search of the house and their leaving her to cope with her fear was a part of the anger he felt. It was too simple to say, she's a carrier so she's guilty and we have the right to do what we like. But he could see her face and her fear as she stood backed up against the wall in the room with Twiss in the window. And him and the woman and their guns, and enough in them to slice her across the middle. And he knew that she'd seen in Twiss's face the desire to fire.

'Thugs in uniform,' some said, and in a way they were right. But someone had to go and do it. Someone had to stop the bombers and the terror in the streets and if the army didn't, who in hell would? But all the time he could see the woman crouched against the rough plaster of the wall and her tired face. She may have been a carrier but perhaps she had been pushed to it. The farm was poor, the prospects not good and the soldiers came into her house and searched, pulled out drawers, looked at the secrets of a trivial little life and walked away. They could forget it, for it was all part of a daily routine. But for that woman it was more. It was a moment when she was tipped over one edge or another, Adams thought. That moment when she backed off to the wall. The moment she realized that he was softening her up with the chat, that was the moment she changed and began to be really afraid. His fault then. Now, 'them up there' wouldn't give a monkey's for the woman, any more than they'd give a toss for the few kids who'd got shot or blown up and died. Just like the bloody IRA.

'Shouldn't be on the streets. . . .' He'd heard an officer say that to someone or other. Jesus wept! A seven-year-old boy wiped off the earth with an accidentally fired round, and all the man would say was, 'Parents should know better, should keep them off the streets.' Adams stared, unseeing, at the ceiling and Tsai didn't touch him now.

'Well?' she murmured.

He shook his head.

'That kid. It's him, isn't it?'

Adams nodded once. If she wanted to think that was all it was, let her think it. He didn't want to talk about the woman in the farm. Not now, not at all.

'Don't go back, Terry. Please stay with me.'

He shook his head. 'I can't,' he said. 'I have to go back. Today. Sorry.'

'Why?' she asked.

'I'm good at it. I've got mates. I've done three tours in Ireland with them. The Creggan, Armagh, Derry . . . all over. I'm doing something.'

'What?' she asked. 'What are you doing but frightening people, children, women. . . . What else do you do?'

164

Terry looked at her. He was bewildered by the question. 'I don't like the bull, Tsai, the training. I'm good, though, when it's all happening. See?'

Tsai turned away from him and pulled the sheet closer around her curled body.

'Your mother and your father,' she said quietly. 'They make me very lonely. They are still shocked you married me. I see their faces every night. I'm different. They don't say so to my face. But I know what they think. See?' she said quietly. They lay in silence for a moment.

'I'm a soldier. I do what I'm told. You knew about soldiers when we married,' Terry said eventually.

She nodded a little. She only had one more thing to say to him. 'My father was killed by a soldier like you. I understand both sides. And you promised we'd be together. I don't want to wait.'

She rolled across to him and pulled him gently down to kiss her. But it would be no use, Adams knew that. That dead kid would see to it and the tired, pale-faced woman crouched against the wall of a house below a road through a dark pine forest, facing two soldiers and terrified.

It'd be no use at all.

Mayhoe was ready to go. It'd been a good leave until last night when it went sour on him. He still didn't really understand what had happened. They'd been dancing every night, and she'd cooked the food he liked and she'd enjoyed bed with him and now suddenly she tells him goodbye.

'I was gonna write, Johnny. Honest to God. But I'll tell you.'

'Shurrup,' he said. 'Just shurrup. Dear John. Dear John, piss off, I don't want to know. You were gonna write to me, and that bastard eyepassin' me at the dance last night. Yeah?'

She rolled across to him. 'No way, Johnny. Not him.

165

Not anyone, Johnny. Honest to God, not anyone. Believe me.'

He looked down at her face as he sat on the edge of the bed and shook his head. 'No way,' he said.

He'd known Joan a long time, since she was a kid almost, and they'd been together since she was fifteen. She was a beautiful girl all right. Slightly slanting eyes in a broad strong face, hair in braids and a figure that was tight and firm. He looked down at her lying naked in the bed and wondered how he'd manage without that body to look forward to.

She looked away and covered herself up quickly.

'You know what it's like here, Johnny. Round here. The police harass us. Oh, yes, they do, you know that.' He shook his head.

'Not me, love,' he said.

'Me. And the others. Listen, Johnny, you're black, right?'

'What the hell do you mean?' he said.

'You're going back to the army. A soldier,' she said.

'Sure. I'm a soldier. What's this about?' He still didn't understand what had happened. 'What d'you want? The ringlets, the Haile Selassie pictures all over the walls? Is that what you want?'

Johnny was angry. They'd been arguing all night and they'd got no place.

'I want you to think about it,' Joan said. 'You're a soldier, fighting, killing other people. All right. But one day it could be a brother, right?'

Mayhoe got up from the bed, walked across the room to the window and looked out down the grey slate roof and across the other grey roofs slippery with rain and green with mould and moss.

He turned back to the girl lying watching him from her bed.

'One day, love, it could be anyone. I just do a job. I

166

don't want to be on that street out there, hanging about the corner waiting for something to drop in my lap. I get paid. I do the job. I get no hassles.'

She laughed scornfully. 'Oh, no?' she said.

He walked across and looked down at her. 'Listen, someone eyepasses me, I don't have to lift a finger. Someone calls me nigger, I don't have to shake my fist even. It's something. My mates do it.' He could see that she didn't believe him. She turned away. He leaned across her and pulled her to face him.

'Any aggravation about being what I am, who I am, I have a man I can talk to. That's what it's about. The man over me and the man over him. You think anyone gives a monkey's what colour you are up a street in Derry? None of my mates ever bothered. I do the job and I'm good at it. That's all.'

She sat up and screamed at him. 'You're Uncle Tomming. You know it when you think about it.'

He stared at her and she waited for him to say something. He sighed a moment and walked away from the bed.

'I don't think about it. Who the hell's been getting at you?'

She tried a softer line. 'Johnny, you're black round here. The police, they double-check and check again. They lift you for loitering just if you stop to look in a shop window. You're part of that, right?'

He smiled. 'I'm not part of that any more. I left.'

'Yeah,' the girl agreed. 'You left and every time you come back you walk these streets and everyone knows Johnny Mayhoe's a soldier. They know that. And you don't have to live here, do you? There isn't anyone else. Just you. But I have to stay back here when you go away, Johnny.'

She was sitting up now and hugging her knees to her breasts. She was desperate for him to understand her, and

167

in his way he did.

'I'm not leaving the army. No way. I leave the army, what do I get? I'll tell you. I get the back of the queue, right? Sorry, mate, the job's filled. It isn't, but they don't want a nigger. No chance on this street. None worth a light.'

'But, Johnny, the army's theirs. Not for us. Not for you. You're . . .' Mayhoe interrupted her.

'You think the white blokes aren't the same, making the best of a bad job? Twiss, Adams, Gadd with his busted leg, all in my section. Some may be in because they want to, but there's one hell of a lot in because it's all there is. I'm a good soldier - I think I am. OK, so some call me Sambo or Jomo and that isn't easy to take. But it's only mates who dare and let anyone else try it. I'd rather be in than on that fucking street, marked for trouble. Oh, yeah . . . and that's not just me, that's whitey too! 'Be a professional,' all that bull. Some believe it. I'm one.'

She stared disbelievingly at him and finally lay back. She didn't bother to cover her breasts or her belly as she lay staring at him and whispered, 'For them, Johnny. Uncle Tom.'

He shrugged and fastened the lock of his suitcase.

'I didn't choose the scene here. I just found a way out of it. And to tell the truth, I don't mind it. I'm staying in.'

'And me?' she asked. He looked across at her for a moment and then shrugged.

'You'll have to do without, if that's what you want, that's all,' he said and he bent to pick up his bags. 'You coming to the station, you'll need to get dressed.'

For a moment she looked across the room at the serious face of her man. She eventually shook her head, turned her back and lay still.

Mayhoe waited a moment and then reached into his pocket and took out a bundle of money. He put three notes on the bed.

168

'Pay the rent,' he said and picked up his bags and walked out.

The Judas gate was so narrow that each of the three soldiers had to ease through it. Johnny Mayhoe and Terry Adams stepped carefully after the colour-sergeant.

Adams looked back to Mayhoe and grinned nervously. He didn't like the idea of sorting out another bomb. They made him edgy and he didn't like the feeling. You never knew what the bastards had done with their bombs these days. They had anti-handling devices and secondary booby traps and the rest down to a fine art. And Frank had it down even finer. He was the best.

'Two, this is six zero bravo. Over.' Jacko was speaking into the handset, just to establish contact. They would keep the net open in case they found anything.

Outside the line of sheds were stacked the empty drums that would eventually be filled with paint, turpentine and thinners. They stood in stacks three men high and stretched right down the yard. To their right the small office block was a shambles of knocked-together rooms in what had been a row of private terraced houses. It'd be a nightmare to search and every step inside would be a dangerous one. It was so easy to booby trap a door or a desk or a floorboard, and so hard to detect.

'We are going into the sheds now. If it's anywhere, it'll be where the paint and stuff is. Out.'

Jacko nodded to the two men behind him. They advanced across the yard in short bursts, leapfrogging each other and giving cover to each other. In a place like this one sniper could take hours to winkle out and they were sitting ducks in the open spaces between the ranks of metal drums.

Suddenly there was a blaze of light as two axe lamps were set up on the outside wall of the stores. The three soldiers inside dived for cover on a reflex. After a moment

Jacko yelled angrily into the handset, 'Six zero bravo, give us a bloody warning next time you do anything. You found the caretaker yet? Over.'

'Two. Not yet. Out.'

Jacko swore. They needed the caretaker. He'd know exactly where the biggest concentration of inflammable material was. He'd know how to reach it without them blundering about the place like blind men and he'd know too if there was much in the store at the moment.

Jacko didn't fancy going up like a human torch if the paint started burning. He grinned across at Adams and Mayhoe, who were pressed against the wall of the first long store shed. He pointed at the rows and rows of steel shelving and lifted his eyebrows in mock despair. Johnny Mayhoe grinned and Adams nodded and looked back the way they had come. The judas gate was opening and Sergeant-Major Gilby appeared with the reluctant caretaker. They walked quickly across to the colour-sergeant.

'He didn't want to come,' said Tom Gilby.

'You've no right to bring me back in this place,' the man interrupted. 'It's a danger to us all if there's anything in there. It'll go up like the biggest thing since the Towering Inferno, mister. Believe me, it would. You've no right to have me back here.'

'Shurrup,' said Jacko. He turned to look at the buildings they had to search.

'I want to know two things,' he said. 'First, where is the main storage area? And second, what's the quickest way to it?'

The man was anxious to get out of the place. He was scared rigid and he knew very well what he had to fear. He pointed along the rows of shelves and gestured to the right. 'Along there, Sergeant, and then right and left. There's a big bay with the main store tanks. You have to get through a couple of other rows of shelving like this. You'll not

170

miss it. Can I go?'

Gilby looked at Jackson, who nodded. 'Hang onto him, Tom,' he said to the sergeant-major. 'I might want to ask a few more questions when we get there. If we get there.'

The sergeant-major and the eager watchman went back across the open space to the judas gate and left the three soldiers alone.

'I don't know what it'll be like, I haven't a clue what he'll have used. But just look for anything out of place and watch, for Chrissake, watch that you don't touch or tread on anything you don't have to. We'll take a row a piece, OK?' The two soldiers nodded.

'Adams, take this centre aisle. I'll take the left and Mayhoe, you take the right. Take it easy and don't fall over it or this whole street is going up for starters. And so will we.'

The three men moved to the ends of their respective rows of shelving. It seemed to Adams to be a hopeless job. Talk about needles in haystacks. Any of these drums marked 'Thinner', 'Undercoat', 'Gloss', 'High Gloss', 'Paraffin Base', any of them could hold three or four hundred pounds of explosive and any of them could be wired up. He looked along the rows of drums and he felt his heart thudding. He glanced at the rifle he held in his hand and reflected that it wasn't going to be much use if any of them triggered the bomb. Jacko had said it'd be on a trembler, which meant it'd only take a little vibration to trigger it and for contact to be made.

He stepped forward slowly and checked, 'Right, left, floor, forward. Right, left, floor, forward. Right, left, floor, forward.' He could hear Johnny Mayhoe muttering to himself as he walked up the aisle to his left. He grinned as he realized that Mayhoe was stringing together the longest cussing he'd ever heard.

He felt his eyes stinging and only when he pushed his hand up into them did he realize that he was sweating. It

171

was rolling down into his eyes and he felt hungry and cold in the guts. Shit, he thought, it's a bastard, this.

The drums were all colours but of uniform size on his rows. He checked carefully between the rows and along the shelving and slowly walked towards the dark shadows at the end of the stores. The light from the arc lamps on the walls did not penetrate here.

At the end of the aisle Adams paused. He waited for Jacko and Mayhoe to reach the end of their aisles and then joined the colour-sergeant. Adams noticed that the colour-sergeant was sweating just as he had been. For a moment none of them said anything. And then Mayhoe muttered, I'd rather be on the street, Colour. Stuff this for a row of tents.'

Outside in the street Felix called Major Taylor to have a word.

'Look, sir, that thing in the car. It's on a timer, right? Trouble is, I haven't got a clue when it'll go up. No way of knowing.'

'Well?' asked Major Taylor. 'What do I do about that?'

'It's the chaps inside . . . they'll have to get their fingers out, sir, or else I'll have to burn that and we risk it. Either way we can get it wrong.'

The major nodded and walked quickly across to Mr Gilby. 'Sergeant-Major,' he said, 'call them up, will you? Tell them to hurry. This one out here is on a timer and Felix doesn't know when it'll blow.'

'Jesus,' muttered Gilby and began to call up the three men in the paint store.

Tompkins was standing behind the bomb disposal truck as the two officers talked. He understood enough to know that the whole store might go up at any minute. He knew that if the car was the trigger for something bigger inside, the whole street could quite possibly be shattered in the blast. It'd certainly get burned out by all that stuff going up.

172

He looked along the street to the barrier that had been erected by the RUC and saw men from Six Platoon dotted amongst the doorways with their rifles at the ready. He checked along the rows of houses and suddenly saw a curtain move in the old woman's place. She was still there. Forgotten, maybe, by the house-clearing squad that had checked only a few minutes ago. Tompkins didn't know what to do. He watched as the bomb disposal man manoeuvred his 'wheelbarrow' into position alongside the Cortina. Major Taylor was walking briskly towards the double doors of the paint store and Sergeant-Major Gilby scared him. He couldn't approach any one of them.

Tompkins ran quickly across the road to join Twiss, who was leaning against the wall of the stores chewing gum steadily and pointing his rifle calmly along the empty street. He was nearest the car. 'Twiss! Eh, Twiss!' called the young soldier. Twiss glanced at him and then turned back to watching up the street.

'What the old lad d'you want?' he asked.

'That house . . . the old woman . . . she hasn't moved.'

Twiss looked at the soldier again, chewed a couple of times and looked away again. He jerked the end of his rifle aggressively. 'Piss off back to your position, red-arse.'

'But the old woman is still in there. She'll get blown to bits if it goes up.'

Twiss stared at the kid in amazement. What a berk this one was!

'We'll all get blown to sodding bits if it goes up. Use your fucking loaf,' he said. 'She chooses to stay, it's her problem, not mine, mate. Do your job and shurrup moaning about that bird.' He spat out the gum he'd been chewing, hitched his gun higher into the cradle of his arm and pulled down the visor of his riot helmet. No bugger's coming down here to riot, he thought, not with a possible bomb in the place. Still, it might save the eyes if the fucker went up. Not that Twiss was sure about that and now this

173

kid rattling on about the old cow in her house. He looked round and was astonished to see the kid still there.

'Piss off back to your position. Gilby'll have your balls,' said the soldier. 'And forget her. She's asked for it. Not you.'

Tompkins ran quickly back towards Felix's control wagon. As he reached it he could see over the captain's shoulder the picture thrown back by the camera on the 'wheelbarrow'. It was scanning the inside of the car and as it scanned the young soldier saw that the ignition key was still in place.

Slowly the scanner took in the rest of the interior, until the picture was locked on the parcel in the back seat.

Tompkins began to work his way back towards Twiss and the blue Cortina.

Inside the sheds Colour-Sergeant Jackson and the two soldiers had already checked three more rows of shelving. At each step they took they stopped and double-checked all around and then moved on carefully again. At the end of the third row they found the narrow corridor that led to the main loading bay. The corridor itself was lined with vats standing on end, and none of them was marked. It was impossible to tell what was in them, except that the place stank of spirit and inflammable vapours.

'Two, this is six zero bravo. We are approaching the main storage area now. Over.'

'Two, Roger.' Major Taylor's voice crackled through the handset that Jacko was holding. 'Have a care. Out.'

Jacko grinned. 'Jesus!' he said to the other two. 'Have a care, the man says.' The three of them moved slowly in single file down the narrow gap between the drums. The dim light was fading fast now and they knew that they had to find something soon or Felix was going to have to burn the car out and be done with it. It was a chance they'd have to take.

The arc lights lit up the whole of the street around the

174

blue car. At the far end of the street two fire tenders stood ready beside the RUC cars. The Land Rovers of B Company blocked off each end of the street and the people who refused to move further away, were crowded up against the barriers, facing the RUC men and the silent soldiers of Six Platoon.

A thin drizzle was drifting across the town and the lights reflected off the sheen of water covering the broken pavements.

The only sounds that could be heard were from the radio communications in the Land Rovers and from the bomb disposal truck, an occasional crackle of voices relaying messages to and from the scene. The 'wheelbarrow' stood against the suspect car and the bomb disposal officer checked the foggy pictures it was relaying back to his screen.

A couple of local pressmen were having a field-day taking photographs and waiting for the big bang that would give front-page stories for the next morning. One of the reporters tried to walk down past the line of soldiers. He was stopped, and turned back protesting that he had a job to do and they were preventing him from doing it. No one said anything further to him but a look at the grey faces of the soldiers and their rifles persuaded the reporter that he'd be better amongst the crowd on the other side of the barriers.

Twiss and the rest of his section had moved back from the area around the Cortina into a safer zone on the orders of the company commander. Major Taylor wasn't going to risk losing men at this stage in their duty tour.

Tompkins edged across to Twiss as he crouched in the shadow of a doorway.

'Someone ought to get that car away,' he said.

Twiss stared at the soldier just out of depot. 'Oh, yeah?' he said.

'If it goes up, that old woman . . .' went on the boy.

175

Twiss laughed. 'You driving it, are you, sunshine? Get stuffed.' Tompkins looked at the coarse, grinning face of the older soldier and then looked away.

He was afraid now, just as they'd promised him when he first came out. He wondered if people like Twiss were ever scared. Down the street he could see Major Taylor and the bomb disposal captain talking together. He wanted to tell them about the woman but he didn't think they'd listen to him.

'I'll have to give it a go,' said Felix. 'Wait much longer and I'll have to burn it and then God alone knows what'll happen.' He was already getting into his protective clothing as he talked. Major Taylor didn't envy him the job. Taking any bomb to pieces was dangerous enough but to take one of Frank's little toys to bits was very close to suicidal. It was a chance the man knew he had to take, however.

The captain picked up his tape recorder and his kit and began to walk towards the Cortina.

'Keep them all back,' he called to Major Taylor. 'And tell your lads inside to come out and get up the street. Just in case.'

The signaller in Taylor's Land Rover yelled across the street.

'Sir! Sir!'

Taylor turned and ran back to the Land Rover and the bomb disposal captain waited where he was.

Inside the stores Jackson, Adams and Mayhoe were standing very still indeed. Adams had spotted it. Just one single coil of wire tucked away at the side of a large drum near the main storage bay.

'Jesus wept,' whispered Mayhoe.

Jacko was already talking into his handset.

'Hello, zero, this is two. We've found it. It's big. Very big.' The wire wound into one drum and out of it into a second on the other side of the shelving. The two drums

176

would hold as much as five hundred pounds of explosive easily and that'd make a very big bang.

'We're coming out,' said Jacko. 'Tell Felix, will you?'

He listened for a moment to the crackling voice of the major and grimaced at what he heard.

'Wilco. Out,' he said and turned, grim-faced, to the other two. 'We're to wait. Till he gets to us with his gear. Sorry about that,' he said, and grinned.

'Not so sorry as we are, Colour,' said Adams.

The three men backed slowly away from the wired-up drums until they could no longer see the tell-tale wires.

Adams rubbed the sweat out of his eyes again and glanced across at Mayhoe. Mayhoe's face was a dull dark grey and Adams knew that Mayhoe was as scared as he was.

'There's one consolation,' Jacko breathed. 'If it does go up we'll not know much about it.'

Jacko checked his watch. They'd been in the stores for exactly twenty-five minutes.

Chapter Ten

Jacko was driving. The children were sleeping in the back and Mary sat quietly beside him. He began to whistle tunelessly. The sunshine lay across the river valley and sparkled off the grass and the spasmodic clumps of oaks and beech trees. Sheep grazed contentedly along the sides of the valley and the drystone walls were well-kept. Each gate post they passed was painted white and the English countryside was prosperous and pleasant to look at.

He stopped whistling and looked across at Mary, who was watching him with a grin on her face.

'Relieved?' she said. 'I know you, Jacko. Mum never learns, does she?'

Jacko grinned too, and watched the road ahead.

'She can't help that,' he said. The break had done Mary good, he thought. Maybe she and her mum don't get on too well but at least she's got the last tour out of her system and she won't be going back there for a long time.

Mary leaned back in her seat and adjusted the sun-visor to shade her eyes. Leave had been all right but her mother had certainly not made it easy. Dad was fine. She was his favourite daughter, she knew that, and he had begun to enjoy Jacko's visit. He was made to think, at least, because Jack was so direct and straight. It wasn't something he was used to and it did seem to stimulate her father. It was sad, though, to see how old he had become over the past eighteen months.

She knew how much Jacko used to dread these duty visits and she was grateful that he came with less fuss than he used to make. Perhaps he felt the need for something that was divorced from their lives in the army. She settled herself more comfortably. She was married to the army, no doubt of that. It wasn't something that she relished but it was fact. And if she was married to it then she was determined to get the best out of it for both of them.

'This command, Jacko,' she said.

She hadn't discussed it since he'd told her at the beginning of leave. She'd waited to let it develop in his own mind first. Jacko took his time about new situations and new places. He'd had enough time now to have made up his mind.

'What about it? I thought you weren't bothered,' he said.

She detected the bitter note in his voice and smiled to herself.

'He's been upset by that,' she thought. 'Perhaps we should have talked earlier.'

'Commanding a platoon, Jacko, it's what they give kids from Sandhurst. You've got twelve years' time in. You're not a kid. What's so great about it? What's so exciting?'

He shook his head. It wasn't easy to explain, even to himself.

'I'm a soldier, a private soldier, Mary. I came . . . you know what I come from. I joined the army as a boy. Right? It's all I'm good at. I am good at it. I like the life. I like the regimental stuff too. I believe in all that. I'm not ashamed to say I'm regimental.' She was laughing. 'What's so bloody funny?'

She shook her head at him.

'You,' she said. 'Defending yourself. Just answer the question, love.'

'I am answering it,' he said. It wasn't something that you could explain to any woman, was it? Loyalty to other men, loyalty to a regiment, a history, a tradition. It blotted out the lack of background.

'They offer me that command - temporary, sure it is. They offer it, that means they've got an eye on me. That's what it means. Partly.' How can you explain to a woman the kick you get out of making them a solid unit, giving

179

them pride, discipline, all those virtues that Jacko regarded as necessary for a reasonable standard and way of living? 'I want to command that platoon, that's all,' he said simply.

'Yeah,' she-said. 'And what about Tom Gilby?'

'What about him?' She had a knack of putting her finger onto the trouble spots instantly.

'You know what about him, Jacko. He's trouble. He looks after Thomas Gilby and you'll be under his thumb and yet not under his thumb. Is that going to be easy? You, a platoon commander, same problems and responsibilities as a junior officer?'

Jacko changed gear and swerved out past a low-loader lorry and back in front of him fast. He nodded and grunted acceptance of what she had said.

'He is company sergeant-major and he carries a lot of clout, does Tom,' she went on. 'Close to the company commander, right? They get on.'

He looked at her in surprise. How on earth did she glean these pieces of information? He sometimes felt that she knew more than he did about the in-fighting in the regiment.

'They do get on, Jacko. Think the same, maybe. Taylor's rigid, likes things set and tickety-boo, as Daddy would say. Thomas Gilby is the same. You stick out like a sore thumb, don't you? Colour-sergeant IC a platoon. Not usual.'

'It happens a lot now. No young officers coming in. Few, anyway.' She nodded.

'So they find it convenient to make you up on a temporary basis and as soon as some red-arse . . .' She saw his surprised look when she used the term. 'I know the words, Jacko. I've been in long enough, haven't I? When some red-arse comes along you move over and he takes the platoon on. You lick it into shape and he takes it on. What happens to you then? NCO without a command. You'll be

180

spitting blood.'

She was right, of course. It wasn't going to be easy to adjust if that happened and the chances were that it would happen. He knew too that she was right about Tom Gilby. But it was a chance he couldn't turn down. She knew that, surely she did?

'What do you want me to do, then?' he asked.

'You've made up your mind, Jacko. You're doing what you want to do. But you're not looking ahead. Not looking to the future. All you can see is those thirty good men and true standing admiringly watching tall, dark, handsome Colour-Sergeant Jackson with crowns and stripes and God alone knows what up your arm. That's what you can see.'

'That's bloody not true!' he said angrily. She was right, of course. He grinned across at her and she put a hand on his thigh as he drove on through the small market town and out into the open hillsides of North Yorkshire. 'Sorry,' he said.

'No, my fault. I shouldn't have said that.'

He sighed. 'In a way you're right. I've been thinking about the job. One thing at a time. You know me. Do one thing right and then move on to the next.'

'But what is next?' she asked, having got him to the point she wanted him at.

'The clever bitch,' he thought admiringly. 'She's been leading round to it again and I didn't see it.'

'I'll not taking a commission,' he said. 'No chance.'

'So?' she said. 'What'll you get, then? Company sergeant-major like Tom Gilby and a life in admin, later if you're not shoved out? What's that?' She was bitter and she couldn't understand Jacko's built-in aversion to taking a position in the commissioned ranks. She didn't understand the automatic, reflex rejection of what they stood for. He wouldn't feel at home in their mess, nor in their company all the time. Much more, he would miss the free-wheeling social life of the Sergeants' Mess. They had

181

their formality in just the same way as the officers. They had their dinner nights and guest nights and all the rest, but they were in the Sergeants' Mess through habit and not because of accident of birth, privilege or the school you went to. He knew that was a simplification of what happened now but it still held good and he didn't want any part of it.

'I'm not taking any commission. I'm going to make . . . well, something else I want,' he said and she noticed from the whiteness of his knuckles as he gripped the steering-wheel that he was more angry than she had meant him to be.

They drove on in silence for a time.

Eventually Jacko spoke again. 'I hope your dad wasn't too upset last night. I cut him off a bit short. He wanted to talk about that kid, what's his name? . . . Tompkins. The one who got . . . you know. I didn't want to talk about it. Your dad just doesn't know what he's talking about. That's it,' he said.

'He has an opinion. He does have that. He has a right to it, Jacko.'

'I just do the job, Mary. That's all I know,' he said. 'I see.' She was very quiet now. He didn't look at her. 'That gets you out of any responsibilities, does it? You don't have to think about it. Just do it blind and hear, see and say nothing. Is that what it is?'

'You do, Jack. You do just the same. Justify what the army does, right or wrong. That's not loyalty, that's blindness.'

'No,' he said quietly. 'Look, we're a group, a club, if you like. In a dangerous situation and targets for anger and hatred and all the rest. Right? We're told to keep law and order and that's a joke. I think it's a joke because we aren't given the power to do it properly, and because the hate-mongers are at work, openly rousing the people to hate even more. Put some of them away and we'd be OK. But

182

no, they're part of the established order here and they're 'untouchable, OK? I'm cynical because I see . . . I see that kid, say, for example. I see him, what was left of him, dumped into a sack in bits, and when it happened the people at the end of that street just drifted away as if they'd been watching a dog fight or a couple of drunks tongue-lashing each other. It didn't mean that to them.' He snapped his fingers. 'So it's no wonder we're cynical, as you say. It's no wonder that we're sick and tired of them all. And of the hate and the destruction and . . . That's our greatest asset. We don't hate any of them. Not unless they kill one of ours and then we do. Oh, yeah. If I could find Frank, that bomber, now I'd, I'd . . .' He stopped talking and sniffed and stared down the long, winding road.

The wreckage had been strewn all across the road. Tompkins had risked all their lives and he'd been every sort of sodding fool. He'd broken the rules, risked something enormous and lost his life to no end. 'Useless. Dead heroes,' he said. 'Bloody useless.'

Mary sat still and quiet and they didn't talk for a time as he drove on south for Salisbury Plain and the barracks.

As Sergeant-Major Gilby drove through the gates past the Wessex Rangers sign a distant clock was chiming nine. He was first back, which was how he liked it. He stepped out of his car, straightened himself and watched as a soldier walked slowly between the two barrack blocks opposite him. The soldier had been left behind with the skeleton staff to man the barracks while the rest got their leave.

For a moment Gilby watched the slouching figure and then he shouted across the square.

'Soldier! Come here.' The soldier looked up, startled, and then began to run across the tarmac to the sergeant-major. He stopped in front of Tom Gilby, who looked awkward and out of place in his civilian clothes.

183

'Major Taylor back yet?' snapped Gilby.

'No, sir,' said the soldier. 'Captain Simmons? Mr Preece?'

'No, sir,' answered the soldier, and Sergeant-Major Gilby began to feel at home. He smiled to himself and then noticed the soldier watching him, waiting for permission to leave.

'You, soldier, you smarten yourself up. This isn't Toc H. This is the army, sunshine. Get yourself sorted. On your way.' The soldier about-faced and marched smartly away across the sunny square. Tom Gilby watched him for a moment and then took his small grip from the back seat of the car and walked to his quarters in the Sergeants' Mess. It was good to be back.

By twelve the bar was crowded. Sergeants and warrant officers mostly still in civvies, were sitting around the room. Sergeant-Major Gilby, now changed into barrack dress, walked through the doors and glanced about the room. Bilinski's back, good, Trotter, good. . . ; No Jackson. Bloody wife held him up, no doubt.

Across the room the RSM smiled at him and beckoned him across. Gilby walked over quickly, exchanging the odd greeting with his platoon sergeants as he went.

'Morning, Tom. Good leave?' asked the regimental sergeant-major. Tom Gilby and he didn't exactly see eye to eye and Gilby knew he had to keep his mouth shut and watch himself if he wanted to get any further. Not that the RSM could put the boot in but he could try if he felt like it and Thomas Gilby didn't want that. The sergeant-major also knew that the RSM had a bitch of a wife, who spent all her time moaning at her husband about the uppityness of the soldiers' wives. She really thought she was in a class by herself. She was a royal pain and they all felt sorry for the RSM on that score.

'Not bad,' he said and tapped the side of his nose.

184

'Cheers.' He lifted his pint.

'What d'you mean, not bad, Tom?'

'Well . . .' Tom Gilby was reluctant to tell anyone about his 'triumphant' leave but he knew that if he told the RSM he wouldn't have to tell anyone else. 'Just between you and me?' The RSM nodded and leaned forward. 'This widow, young widow. She works in a little pub I go to. She's always had a bit of a shine for me and I thought, this time, Tom Gilby, don't look a gift horse, so to say.' He smiled and winked.

'You're a dark horse, Tom, you are. You did it, then. She'll nail you up. I've told you before.'

Tom Gilby smiled. 'Drink up,' he said. 'My shout.'

Jackson and the two soldiers stood at the end of the passage and while they waited they stared at the place where they knew the bomb to be. They were willing it not to go off now, willing it to wait at least until they'd got clear of the building.

They heard the slam of the judas gate in the distance. The bomb disposal man was on his way. Mayhoe glanced at Adams and tried to grin. It didn't work too well.

'Nasty,' said Jacko ironically. 'You did well to spot it.' Adams shrugged and watched the end of the dim passage.

'You all right?' The bomb disposal captain was cheerful enough. 'You'd better show me. You have checked for secondaries, haven't you?'

'Yeah,' said Jackson, 'We checked when we moved back here. And then we just kept very still. Till you got here.'

The captain unslung his gear and began to sort it out. 'It's big,' said the colour-sergeant and the captain glanced up from what he was doing.

'How d'you know?' he asked.   ,

'It's in two bloody great drums, that's how,' said Jackson. The captain nodded, straightened up and turned to

185

them. 'Right, who's going to show me?' he said.

Adams and Mayhoe looked at Jackson and waited for him to volunteer. 'I'll remember that,' he said to them, grinning. They grinned back. Somehow they felt more relaxed now that an expert was here, though why they should feel that the bomb wasn't just as deadly they wouldn't have been able to explain.

The captain and Jackson walked gingerly down the passage with Jackson leading. They stopped at the end where it opened out into the large storage and filling bay.

'There you go,' breathed Jackson to the captain. The captain looked at the bomb carefully without moving for some time. Then he turned back to the colour-sergeant and motioned for him to move back with him.

They reached Adams and Mayhoe and the captain appeared to be surprised to see them still there. 'You don't have to stay. Unless you want to, of course. You can watch if you like,' he said.

'No way,' said Mayhoe. 'No chance.' The two soldiers looked at Jackson, who nodded. 'On your way, lads, and take it easy.'

Take it very easy, and don't slam the door on your way out. That bastard's on a trembler and a vibration will set it off. OK?' said the captain. The two soldiers nodded and moved fast down the dim corridors and out into the evening light beyond the store sheds.

The captain was already talking into his tape recorder. 'Trembler device, located inside shelving and to be activated by smaller car bomb outside the factory. Inflammable in drums all round. Probably Frank's. It's ingenious enough . . . probably wired in series, if he runs to form.' The bomb disposal man looked at Jackson. 'You want to stay, Colour?' Jacko shook his head. 'It's going to be a bastard to get at, Colour. And I don't have a lot of time. If that bloody car goes up outside it'll trip that trembler sure as eggs is eggs. It's neat, isn't it? A series of small bombs and you think that's all you've got and suddenly bingo, this one.' He sighed and pulled down the visor on his helmet. 'Can't even get much of the gear on, not in that sort of space.'

Jackson saw that he'd discarded his armoured suit and that the only protection the man had was the visor for his eyes. It wouldn't much matter, he thought, not if that one went up. Even in a suit you'd roll out like raspberry jam - if they found anything to roll out.

'Good luck, sir,' he said and walked quickly away, leaving the man alone with his bomb.

Adams and Mayhoe stepped through the Judas gate into the street and blinked in the glare from the arc lights that were blazing down from the wall around the stores and from the Land Rovers, fire engines and police cars parked at both ends of the street.

Sergeant-Major Gilby stood with Major Taylor as the men walked quickly across to report.

'Well?' asked Major Taylor. 'What does he think?'

'He says it's big and it's nasty. We didn't stop for any more, sir,' said Adams. 'It was a bit of a bastard to find, sir. Tucked away. On a trembler, he said.'

Gilby sucked his teeth. Frank was a clever bastard all right, and he'd nearly had them all for patsies. If they'd blown that car they'd have burned down half a street, not to mention the warehouses and stores further down the road. Jacko pushed through the gate and walked briskly across.

'He's starting work now, sir,' he said. 'He doesn't reckon he's got a lot of time. Frank is a devious bastard. That's what he thinks, sir. He'll make a report as he goes along, he said. On the net.'

They walked across to the Land Rover to pick up the messages that were coming through from inside the stores. Gilby nodded at Adams and Mayhoe. 'You did well. Good lads. Not easy going in there. I'll see you after.' He smiled

187

tightly at them and turned to join the major and Colour-Sergeant Jackson.

Adams looked at Mayhoe and shrugged. 'I'll see you after. Stuff him,' he said and jerked his head in the direction of the houses.

'The last doorway we can find, Johnny. That's for us.' They moved briskly down past the fire crews and the RUC constables and through a couple of groups of soldiers who asked questions and got nothing for answers. The two soldiers intended to make themselves as secure as possible.

'Eh, Tompkins!' Adams yelled at the soldier who was standing by himself in the middle of the street, staring down towards the factory gates. 'Get yourself in cover, mate. It's the biggest bugger I've ever seen. Five hundred pounds if there's one.' Tompkins didn't respond and after a moment Adams walked on with Johnny Mayhoe.

Tompkins was gazing at the blue Cortina. He knew if it went up that the old woman would die, and he didn't want that to happen. Six Platoon was grouped at one end of the street, facing the silent crowd beyond the barricades; Major Taylor, Sergeant-Major Gilby and Colour-Sergeant Jackson were at the command Land Rover. Only Sergeant Bilinski and Twiss were between him and the car.

He walked quickly along the street to join Twiss who was stolidly chewing another piece of gum.

'Got a fag?' asked Twiss, and Tompkins shook his head. 'Useless, you are,' muttered Twiss, and he settled back against the wall and stared, unseeing, across the dark shadow and into the sharp pool of light on the other side of the street. 'That old woman . . .' Tompkins began.

'Stuff her, mate. There's a bloke in that place working on the big one now, right? I'm not going across any street for any poxy woman, mate. If that bloody thing blows we'll all be roman candles, right?'

Tompkins's hands were sweating. He was cold in the gut and his legs felt as if they weren't with him. He

188

sniffed, shut his eyes for a moment and then he began to run.

At the bomb disposal vehicle they could hear the stream of comment from the bomb disposal man as he worked on the delicate task of unwiring the detonator from the explosive.

'Last bit now . . . trembler is steady. Two wires . . . I've found no hidden circuit . . . Wait . . . wait . . . the clever bastard. Hold on.'

Sergeant-Major Gilby could feel the sweat building on his forehead. Jackson drew in his breath and Major Taylor began to tap nervously on the dashboard of his Land Rover.

Felix was working deftly and almost without thought. The trembler arm was dead still but he knew that the slightest knock would touch a contact on either side of the arm and that'd be that. The hidden circuit he had found had been skilfully concealed along the back of the shelving and he'd very nearly missed it. He knew that if he stopped to think about that his hands would begin to tremble and he had to keep working, not think. If he thought they were all dead anyway. He'd already done too many bombs this tour. Sometimes a man working on them could almost become addicted to the adrenalin that pumped through when he began to work on a bomb. He disconnected the last wire of the secondary circuit and glanced at the trembler. It was steady.

'All right. Secondary circuit gone. Hidden behind the shelving. Cunning bugger, our Frank. It is his work all right. No doubt of it. Got his mark on it. I'm cutting the first circuit.'

As he reached for the sharp-nosed pliers in his belt Tompkins was causing panic outside in the street. He had run fast and low across the brightly lit area near the Cortina, he had ripped open the door and started the car almost before anyone realized what he had done. It was the

189

noise of the engine that brought everyone to their feet and then prompted every man to run for cover. Tompkins wrenched the car round in a tight turn and drove fast for the far end of the street. Six Platoon scattered fast and hit the ground, crawling as they did so, looking for cover. The car picked up speed and made for the barriers at the end of the street. As it went through them there was a searing explosion. The car had just begun to turn the corner and the end house took the main blast. Almost immediately after the first explosion a second ripped the car in two and the hot, jagged metal began flying, embedding itself in whatever it hit. Luckily the few people left at that end of the street had run to join the soldiers and were protected by the end house. Tompkins had no protection. The bomb which had been placed on the back seat burned through the seat and then through his back. It ripped his stomach across and his body began to disintegrate before the second explosion shattered the car and everything inside it. He'd tried. The petrol tank exploded. He knew nothing.

At the moment of the first explosion Felix snipped the wire. He heard the blast and he watched desperately for the trembler to contact. It tipped, dipped, touched its contact plate, and the captain waited and waited, and the trembler flicked back into position again. Nothing went up. He'd do another one tomorrow.

'I'll coming out,' he said angrily. 'That bastard car shouldn't have gone up. He was sure he'd had a safety margin and that it wasn't due to blow for some time. Frank must've put another in the car as well. The crafty bastard.

His hands began to tremble. He shoved them into his pockets and walked quickly away from the drums full of explosive and the cut wires and the useless trembler at the back of the drum.

For a few seconds no one moved in the street. The dull pall of smoke hung heavily in the damp evening air and the shattered ruin of the car smouldered.

Gilby moved first. 'Wait!' he yelled at the soldiers, who were crouched against the wall, in doorways, and behind the Land Rovers. He walked gingerly across the street and down towards the burning car. He stood by it for a moment, blinded by the smoke that covered what was left. Then he turned fast on his heel and walked away. No one said anything for a moment.

'Stupid bastard,' muttered Twiss as the sergeant-major walked past him. Gilby appeared not to have heard the soldier. Major Taylor met the sergeant-major in the middle of the street.

'Well?' he asked.

'Hell,' said the sergeant-major.

'He's dead, sir,' said the major.

'Bastards,' muttered the angry soldier. He turned towards the other end of the street, where the crowd was already collecting again to see what had happened.

'Twiss!' yelled the sergeant-major. 'Clear those bastards off the street. All of them. Get them off the street and out of my sight. Two Section, go with him. Box, Corporal Box . . . you're in charge. Any aggro, sort it.' He was white with anger. That stupid, bloody, wet-eared brave lad. Just out and doing a fucking idiot trick like that . . . Gilby was shaking with anger now. Two Section moved fast up the street and the crowd melted away.

'Sergeant-Major,' called Major Taylor. 'We'll get it hosed down. Do what you have to do.'

Gilby turned away to the fire engines and signalled them closer. They turned their hoses on and began to spray the car. Steam drifted up into the damp air and with it the stink of burnt flesh.

Jacko walked across to the sergeant-major. 'What happened?' he asked.

Gilby pointed to the wrecked car. 'He drove it away. The lad. He drove it away. No one saw him. He just got in

191

and drove it away. Tompkins was his name, wasn't it? Playing bloody heroes. Useless.'

Jacko swore softly and walked across the street. They'd stopped hosing the car now and soft dribbles of water and steam hissed out of the wreckage. Holding the steering-wheel Jacko saw a hand, just the kid's hand, and the steering-wheel was lying in the gutter where the stinking, dirty water ran away down the drain.

'Jesus wept,' he said and turned away. It was a soft evening and the drizzle fell softly across the town as they began to search for bits of the lad that they could decently bury.

Across the road from the fir trees the farmhouse was in darkness when the troops arrived. Jacko and Bilinski went in first and were followed by Two Section and some of recce section.

The house was empty. They searched it top and bottom and there was no one left. In the bedroom there was the sickly smell of perfume. The angry soldiers thudded back down the stairs into the front room.

'Not a thing,' said Adams. 'Empty. Same downstairs, Colour?' Colour-Sergeant Jackson nodded. 'She's gone, yeah.'

'We were set up. She set us up. I'll lay odds,' said Adams.

Jackson looked at the angry soldier a moment and suddenly felt sorry for him.

'Would you tell if you were her, if you were one of them?' he asked. Adams shook his head in impotent rage. They killed a kid. Tompkins was a kid,' he yelled.

'Yes,' said Jackson quietly. 'And he forgot the rules, didn't he? Stupid.'

Adams kicked the table across the room. 'It's not that. It's not that, is it? Eyes shut, hands behind your back. If you see the man you want smile at him. Pat him on the head and wait till he kills someone before you knock him

192

off. Before you knuckle him, even. It's that.'

Jackson sighed and stared around the darkening room.

'Whose side are you on, Adams? You want to be like them?'

Adams looked sharply at the tall man beside him. He was so angry he could hardly speak. He tried to clear his head. He kept on seeing the car, the steam drifting up from it, and he kept smelling the stink of flesh.

'I dunno. I just do a job and shurrup, don't I? Am I right?' he asked.

B Company, Wessex Rangers, were standing at ease. Colour-Sergeant Jackson stood a couple of paces ahead of Sergeant Bilinski and behind him the men of Six Platoon waited in the afternoon sun for Major Taylor to finish.

'Glad to have you all back on time. You're a credit to the battalion and I want it to go on like that. You did well in Ireland. No problems, no sweat and progress was made in our area. GOC sent a message, which the CO passed on to me and which I will now pass on to you . . .'

Jacko watched Tom Gilby straighten his back a notch at the mention of the GOC. Jacko smiled. He'd got his command. He'd a good platoon, Twiss, Mayhoe, Adams, Bilinski and the rest. Yates, Baker, Gadd. For a moment Jacko shut his eyes against the glare of the sun. Major Taylor didn't mention the lad who was killed. Jacko knew it was deliberate. It was too soon to talk about him, too soon to think coolly about it. He hadn't known anyone in the company. Hadn't been there long enough. Here today and gone tomorrow, and that bastard bomber sitting in a pub, no doubt, boasting how one of his had got a British soldier.

Jacko opened his eyes as Major Taylor finished. The platoon commanders were to take their platoons for the rest of the afternoon. Jacko turned slowly and looked at Sergeant Bilinski, who was standing ramrod-straight, staring to the front. Jacko glanced along the line of soldiers and he thought again how very young they were. No one flickered, no one moved. Colour-Sergeant Jackson was new to them and they'd not take any chances yet.

The colour-sergeant knew exactly what they were thinking as he gave his platoon their first order.

'Six Platoon . . . Platoon . . .'

The walls of the farm have broken from neglect. No one has ever come back to the house and the rooms are a shambles of rotting furniture, broken glass and damp plaster. The ceiling in the corner of the front room has caved in slightly and the land is untended. The land is desolate, despoiled and ravaged by men. And a rotting sack in a long box holds all that was left of Tompkins, all the battalion has left behind. The rain still drips from the dark pines on the hillside over the farm. It is night again.

— ooOoo —

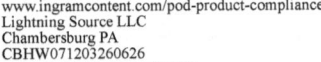